Dirk's

Ancient

Times

Collection

FOR LITERARY HEAT

www.BarbarianSpy.com

This book is copyright © Dirk Hessian 2016
Dirk Hessian asserts his right to be known as the author of this work.
Published by BarbarianSpy in 2016
Cover design © S Bush 2016
Cover image: manipulated © Mega11 | Dreamstime.com
ISBN Print: 978-1-925190-79-3
All rights reserved

BarbarianSpy
Toronto, Australia

Dirk's Ancient Times Collection

by

Dirk Hessian

Table of Contents

Introduction

Dirk Hessian specializes in gay male historical action/adventure novellas and novels. His works are set in a wide variety of historical time periods and event settings from the ancient times of the mystical past through medieval and American history up to modern times worldwide, as far afield from his home setting of the United States as France, Scotland, the Black Sea, and China.

His shorter works, previously available only in e-book form, are now being brought together in print collections. This is the first of that series, including works covering the mystical beginnings of time to the Crusades, *Beginning of Time*, *Labyrinth*, *The Prophecy of Noto*, and *The King's Men*. Coming soon will be his *America's Founding* and *America Divided* collections.

The first book in the collection, *Beginning of Time*, is a mystical story of primeval survival and sexual awakening and fulfillment of "man," represented here by a single young man, struggling to learn how to fit into his hostile, primitive environment. As he moves from ancient civilization to slightly more advanced ancient civilization—not always by choice—his resilience is taxed to overcome his innocent vulnerability until reaching his protector and ultimate lover and having his love story depicted on a cave wall for future generations to decipher and appreciate.

"All of life for those of us with royal blood is risk—a labyrinth," the Second Queen of Phitio tells her precious son, Nyke, in the novella *Labyrinth*. Nyke has been marked for sacrifice the minute the crown prince accedes to the throne of the mystical country of Phitio. And from that moment forward the young Nyke is caught up in a complex web of scheming and double-dealing as, using his wits and his beautiful, lithe, young body and his ability to inflame the lusts of men of power, he works his way through the convoluted posturing and maneuvering of the warring nation states of Phitio, Brixia, Morini, and Cenopolis in an effort to gain the center of the labyrinth—both real and figurative—and to survive to return to Phitio in victory.

In *Prophecy of Noto*, even as the old king of the mythical kingdom of Aram is dying, the Oracle at Noto is giving the prophecy that his progeny will rule as high kings of all of the disparate nations of the region. The stumbling block to this is that his heir, Cletar, is besotted with catamites and will not lay with a woman. At the gate of the castle is a siege army under the command of King Zara of the kingdom of Akamantis on the nearby island of Li'. The king's ancient adviser, the Watchman, devises a plan, which unfolds on a convoluted path over decades, to fulfill the prophecy of the oracle even as the dying king's other four advisers are steeped in their own designs on the throne of Aram and, each for his own reason, determined that the oracle's prophecy will never come to fruition.

Rife with court gossip, complex double dealing and treachery, as well as sexual innuendo and a ménage of couplings, *The King's Men*, inspired by Richard the Lionhearted's conquering of the island of Cyprus during the Medieval crusades, is a gay male romp of how lowly court attendants were able to manipulate and influence major events in the Europe of the Middle Ages.

Beginning of Time

Chapter One: Earliest Time

I have no memory of a beginning. From the time I first had any sense of being alive, all of my efforts were taken up with trying to find enough berries, nuts, and leaves that wouldn't sicken me to make me able to move in the forest and shelter under low-lying branches when the threat of the elements or the Others arose. Even in slaking my thirst I had to learn that the water trickling down from the rocks into the pool was good to drink but that the great body of water lapping up on the edges of the sand and stretching to the horizon would just make me more thirsty and would confuse my mind. But I had to be careful when going to the pool. There could be animals of prey there and there also could be the Others. Some of the Others were animals of prey too.

In my early years finding the berries, nuts, and leaves that would not harm me was a solitary experience—and countless numbers of the Others who I knew were there in the forest with me and were guessing what they ate, as I was, sometimes just no longer were there or I saw as rotting shells on the forest floor. They had taken risks with what they ate and had lost.

What all of the Others—me included—always looked for were those big nuts that nestled under the fanned leaves of the slender, swaying trees near the fringe of sand and forest and sometimes in families of trees further in the forest. One of those nuts could sustain me for several changes of the light to dark and back to light again. At the center was sweet liquid more filling and satisfying than water from the pool. And between that and the brown, hairy outer shell was a white pulp that was the most delicious to taste of all. But this wasn't just my favorite. It was the favorite of all. And unless there were no Others around when one of these fell from the trees of the fanned leaves—or could be shaken down—this, this was when the Others came together. But they weren't coming together in touching or joining. They came together in hisses and fists bunched and claws extended. And they would fight for the prize of the large nut.

For untold time I only knew of the large, sweet nut liquid and pulp from watching the Others fight over it—with sometimes being able to pull away a scrap of it when they weren't noticing as they hissed over the treasure. But in time I became large and strong enough myself to hope to have such a nut for myself—even if I had to fight for it.

This change in how I dared hope for possession of the large nut was my first sense of anything. My first sense of the solitary nature of existence had been when I had fought for the nut and saw that this was different from my earlier aloneness. Before that, I always felt Others being around, but there were no connections. I almost—almost but not quite—could remember a time when there had been another with me. An older one. One who touched me and pulled me back from danger and began my learning in what to eat and drink and what not to—and, just as important, when to step out and when to hide. But I vaguely remember her being there—and then turning and finding her there no more.

Sometimes, as I aged, I noticed two of the Others being close to each Other, joined and making guttural noises. But this was something I only noticed when I started to have feelings to be curious about the Others and what they did—and began to wonder why they were so unconnected, suspicious, and hissing at anyone coming near. But then how they sometimes joined with one becoming inside the Other and both making those strange, but interesting guttural noises.

I wanted to make those guttural noises too. As I grew I wanted to have connections with Others. I didn't want to have to discover what would satisfy my hungers and not sicken me. And when I did discover this, I wanted to share that with the Others. I wanted to touch and to share. What surprised me the most was that I wanted—that I wanted anything. I kept trying to remember, to remember an earliest time. And I could not do so. It was only when my body began to show its wants to me—and especially on the rare occasions that I saw Others joining—that I began to look beyond the gathering of sustenance for my belly alone and started to see the world around me.

And to wonder why.

But until Graybeard came to me, I was like any of the Others. Alone and ever vigilant and just trying to find enough berries, nuts, and leaves and water that would not sicken me from one time of light through darkness and the next time of light.

I was reaching for a rich, purple berry, deep in the forest, when I felt a touch on my forearm. I reached over to brush the insect away but found that it was no insect's touch. It was one of the Others—and not just anyone of the Others. It was the elder, the graybeard. The one I had learned to watch scavenge for food. The one that I instinctively knew understood what to eat and what not to, or he would not be so advanced in age. He was also one who I had seen join with Others—with other of the young, ones who existed before I did. But ones no older than I now was. He had a watering tube longer and thicker than those I saw dangling between the legs of Others, and I had seen him penetrate the holes of Others and make those guttural sounds— and cause the Others being possessed to make those guttural sounds—that made me feel strange and pleasant also. And that made me want to make guttural sounds as well.

Graybeard was grimacing at me. I did not know what he wanted. I was in too much shock that he had touched me. I had no memory—Other than a distant one—of any Other touching me in anything but a struggle over a large, sweet nut. Indeed, I had little memory of another coming this close to me except in a threatening stance to send me away.

I was failing to respond as he wanted, so Graybeard snapped the purple berry from the bush and tossed it away. I understood then. He was telling me that the berry would sicken me. I again was frozen with surprise. Except for that long-ago memory of one who cared for me, I had no experience of any Other teaching me anything about the berries, nuts, and leaves or showing any notice of what I did at all as long as I stayed my distance.

Graybeard wasn't staying his distance, though. Even after he had thrown the poisonous fruit away, he did not take his hand from my forearm. In fact, he was gripping my arm more tightly. And then he was gripping my other arm with his other hand. He was behind me, making those guttural noises I was so aroused by. And I was aroused now too—my body, my own tube—were responding as they had been doing for many changes of light to dark to light. Responding as they did as long as I gripped my tube with my hand and eventually felt the release of the white, sticky fluid from inside me.

I didn't know what was happening. All I knew was that Graybeard and I were having a connection, that my body was aroused, and that I was beginning to make guttural noises that matched his.

He pushed me down on all fours and covered my back with his body—as I'd seen him and Others do when they made those guttural noises. And then I felt the searing pain as he penetrated me, joining with me, entering me and connecting our bodies as I had never connected with another one before. I was being opened and filled with an ever-deepening penetration.

And then, as the pain melted away into a new, strange, and wonderful feeling of two being one and of the guttural sounds having a purpose and reward, I spilled my seed on the ground as Graybeard planted his deep inside me. I learned what this connection was all about.

And I didn't want it to stop.

Nor did it stop. After the time in the forest with the poisonous purple berry, I had another at my side, guiding me and touching me, protecting me and breeding me. I understood what mating was about—and why all that I had gone through in the dullness of time to reach this time was worthwhile.

At the same time the inclusion of my mounting Graybeard in my life gave me a sense of protection and contentment, I realized that I became the object of hostility from some of the Others. Some of the Other young, not much older than I was, taunted me with hisses and made feints of attacks against me whenever I was not at Graybeard's side.

I understood why, though. These had been ones Graybeard had guided and touched and breeded earlier. I recognized some of them from memories of seeing Graybeard couplings in the forest, which were more vivid in my mind now that I knew the heights of pleasure Graybeard's big penetrator brought.

My pleasure also proved to be my undoing—at least for the near future.

It wasn't only the elements and each other that threatened the Others who lived around me. There also was a threat from across the sky-reaching rocks and from the broad waters flowing to the horizon. There were others near us, large, hulky, nasty others who smelled of rotten flesh.

They came to us in wooden vessels across the waters, coming straight out of the golden disk in the sky so that we did not see them until they almost were upon us. I was on the sands between the forest and the water. Graybeard wasn't there. Both one of the Others, the one who had laid with Graybeard before he selected me, was there, inching toward me. Being aware of where he was was what kept me from seeing the approaching vessels holding those I thought of as Sharpspears, because they carried with them long sticks, sharpened at the end. I'd seen them throw these sticks at long distances and bring animals—and, once or twice, an Other—down with them.

I heard the alarm, though, and turned and saw that the lead vessel was nearly where the water met the sand. Three giant Sharpspears were leaning toward the sand, ready to jump out. I turned and ran, but the Other who resented my lying with Graybeard had moved closer to me and I saw the rock he was carrying too late.

When I opened my eyes, I felt the fullness inside me. I was pinned on my back on the sand, with a Sharpspear holding down each of my arms. A third Sharpspear was kneeling between my spread thighs. And he was inside me. Other Sharpspears were standing around watching. And in time, they were all inside me too. I don't know how many before my eyes closed again in saving darkness of eye and mind.

* * * *

As I came out of my stupor, I slitted my eyes to get an idea where I was without revealing that I once more was awake. I knew I wasn't on the sand. I was curled on my side on something hard and curving under me, and I was being rocked. I had to fight hard the urge to turn my belly inside out. At first all I could see were bare legs of brawny men. Then as the stench coming off the men assailed my senses, I realized that I was in a vessel of the Sharpspears, who were paddling us out into the waters, toward the glowing disk on the horizon. I'd never been out on the broad water before. I wanted to moan—and not just from the soreness of having taken so many penetrators, but also from the fear of being on the water. This was nothing like I had known before.

But I had never known anything good before other than Graybeard's attentions, so there wasn't much of a loss to feel.

What I felt was hungry, but I did not believe that there would be any berries, nuts, or leaves for me to eat out here on the water.

One of the Sharpspears nudged me with his foot and grunted, but I pretended not to be aware. I was saving myself, building up my strength. If ever they would come to sands again, I would try to escape them.

I felt the bottom of the vessel rub up against sand, and then the Sharpspears jumped out and started pulling the vessel up onto the sands. I lifted my head enough to get a sense of where we were. We were on a wide ribbon of sand much like the one I came from. At the end nearest to me a large pile of stones tumbled down to meet the sea and make a wall against whatever was beyond. The same barrier marked the far end of the sand area, but there, in the shadow of the rocks was a grouping of piled sticks and straw and moving about these were brown figures—not the Others that I knew—but more Sharpspears.

I bounded out of the vessel and struck out for a dense forest area where the sand met the forest at the rock-marked end of the sands. I glanced around to see that the vessel I was in had been the first to reach the sands, but that more wooden vessels, with three Sharpspears each in them were gliding into across the waters to the sands.

I had caught the Sharpspears in my vessel by surprise, though, and I was well into the dense forest before they reached the forest edge of the sand.

I stumbled through the forest through one dark and well into another light before I felt safe enough to stop and look around for something to quell my hunger and quench my thirst. I found a rivulet of a stream and drank my fill. Then I started searching for berries and nuts. There were a few I recognized and a few I didn't. I was very hungry. After reaching greedily for and eating berries I didn't recognize, my belly heaved and I could not keep what I'd eaten down. I was miserable for the time for a storm of rain and wind to pass over me and I thought that I might never see another change from dark to light. But I slowly felt better.

After that I was much more careful what I picked from the bushes and trees to eat. When I calmed down, I discovered that there was an abundance of berries and leaves that Graybeard had signaled to me I could eat.

When I felt strong again I began to walk toward the lands reaching up for the sky, thinking that perhaps my land of Others—and Graybeard—were on the other side. Before I reached there, though, I came to a large clearing in the forest, where the plants were growing strangely. There were not scattered around naturally but were set in rows and spaced apart from each other.

I walked into the field of plantings to look at them more closely, to determine if the yellowish nubs on them were something that I could eat. So taken was I with looking at the strange plants, though, that I was almost upon the tall, thin breathing figures before I saw them. They stood there, most of

15

them holding woven baskets holding fruits and nuts, not looking threatening, holding their hands out toward me. They were pale of skin and had cloth draped around their waists, hiding their sex. They did not seem to mean me harm, but I turned away from them—only to find that others were gathered behind me, in the direction from which I'd come.

I turned back to see that one of these figures was bending down and breaking off one of the yellowish nubs for a plant and offering it to me. I just stared. But after he had eaten that himself and then broken off another nub and held it toward me, I took that and ate. The taste was pleasant, and I could feel that it would please and fill my belly.

I came to think of these as the Gentle People, for they welcomed me with smiles and open arms.

I went with them down a beaten path leading away from the field and into another clearing, where more of the stick and grass piles were sitting around in a circular pattern around a central place of beaten earth.

As I watched in awe, a giant of a figure draped in a red and yellow cloth appeared as if from magic from one of the piles of grass. This was an elder who was to become the penetrator for me that Graybeard no longer was. He took me into the pile of grass, which I found was hollow inside and soon learned provided shelter from the elements and the cold when it came upon us. This experience was an amazing one for me, as I had always found shelter in the forest, in hollows and under branches, but I never was protected there as I was in these grass piles.

The elder of the Gentle People was surprised and happy to find that I had useful knowledge to share about the berries, nuts, and leaves of the forest just as the Gentle People had knowledge to give to me of the plants that they were growing and taking care of—and storing for the bad times.

The Gentle People were unlike those I had known. They were connected and they shared knowledge and they knew of many comforts that my people did not. And they had sounds and gestures and helped them connect. They were unlike what I had learned of the Sharpspears too. The Gentle People conveyed to me that the Sharpspears smelled as they did and walked with

16

the pointed sticks they had because they were meat eaters. They hunted the animals of the forest with their pointed sticks. The Gentle People, like me, only ate plants. And they lived with—and not against—the animals of the forest.

The Gentle People also liked to touch and connect—again unlike the Others I had grown with. The elder, in particular, liked to touch me. And I found that arousing—and my body told him that I found that arousing. With this knowledge of the effect of his touching on me, the elder took aside his red and yellow cloth and showed me that his body enjoyed the touching of me too. He wanted to touch me on the inside, and I showed to him that I wanted that too.

I learned that there were other ways of achieving the pleasure of the penetrating taking than Graybeard had shown me. Men could do this facing each other, with their lips touching lips and other parts of the body too and with me, the receiver, raising and lowering myself on his penetrating, consuming shaft. I learned that the brown circles on my chest could become hard nubs and bring pleasure when sucked by another. And I learned that when the elder moved his lips over my own penetrator and down the shaft and then up and down again and he gave suck to my nob with his grasping lips, that I found new heights and breadths of pleasure—and one release moving to an even more intense release. It was not long before he was granting me deep moans of his own as I did the same for him.

I fit in well with the Gentle People, and I could not have wished a better way to spin out my days of light turning to dark and back to light countless times.

Chapter Two: Earlier Time

I knew as soon as I was coming close that I should not go on—that there was nothing to go on for. At first I sensed it; everything was too quiet. None of the small animals and birds were about, and the bushes themselves seemed to be holding still in fear. And when I came closer, I could smell it on the air—the fear was there, but also something else. Nothingness.

No, there was no reason to go ahead and every reason not to. I turned and as silently as possible fled back the way I'd come, trying to be as careful as possible not to spill the precious fruit I had been out foraging for from the loosely woven basket I was carrying.

I didn't run far, though. I had heard them, thrashing in the bushes around our clearing, and now that thrashing was coming toward me. I saw a rock outcropping off the path, over toward the cliffs beyond which the Sharpspears lived. Normally I would not go any farther toward where they lived, the Meateater Sharpspears, than this path. But I needed shelter. I needed to hide. And the most likely place for that was by the rock outcropping in the direction of the Sharpspears' cliffs.

I turned off the path and started to move toward the outcropping. But the ground was uneven and hidden by low growth, and I was paying more attention to what was coming my way along the path than to where I was stepping. I placed my foot in a hole and fell, letting out a little cry that I knew might be the death of me. And when I arose, I could barely walk. My ankle was twisted—or worse. And all of the fruit had tumbled out of the basket.

I could hear them approaching, though, and I turned and hobbled as quickly as I could, away from them. I made it to the rocks and found a hollowed-out place, probably some animal's dwelling at some point, and I folded myself into this small space and tried to make myself as one with the rock and the bush as I could.

They were close now, and a chill ran up my spine. I could smell them now. Meateaters. My worst fear. The Sharpspears had come down into the valley. It would mean the end of the Gentle People. Our elders had sung of this. We all knew it was only a matter of time.

All of which meant nothing to me at this exact moment. Even any grieving I could do for my chosen own would have no meaning if I joined them in the next few moments.

And then the likelihood of that happening exploded forth, as I moved my leg without thinking and came down at an odd angle on the already-twisted ankle and gave out a low grunt of pain.

18

The undergrowth came alive with noise, and the branches of the bush were parted, and the face of a feared Meateater and the tip of a sharp spear appeared between the spread branches.

Despite the ankle, I jumped up and ran at an angle away from the ugly face, not feeling the pain in the rush of adrenaline racing through me just to stay alive for a few more moments.

But there was another Meateater of the Sharpspears—a larger and fatter one—before me where I was running. I turned yet again and scrambled along the face of the rock outcropping, trying to slip away from them as the two Meateaters raised their pointed sticks, went into a crouch, and began to close in to me. Their eyes were flashing with excitement, and they were grunting the pleasure of the kill. Their spear points were dripping in blood, blood of my adopted clan, I knew.

But just then there was a bellow from beyond them, and another Meateater, larger by far, all muscle and power, hairy, with a gigantic poker between his legs and a heavy seed sac hanging down below his belly belt burst between the two others. He was wielding a thick, intricately carved and notched cudgel, which he raised menacingly above his head. He spread his arms wide, motioning the other two off, and they crouched down even more, leaned away from him, and backed off like beaten tamed animals.

Making to take advantage of Big Stick's appearance— for this was the name I was to call him to myself, neither of us ever able to converse in anything but grunts and expressions and pointings, I turned again and made to run off to the side, along the face of the rock. But my run was no more than a hobble, and Big Stick's legs were much more powerful than mine.

He reached me easily and grabbed me by the scruff of the neck with his massive, calloused hand and turned me. With a mighty blow, he backhanded my face with the other hand, and my head snapped hard around and I sank down to the earth in a daze.

The starbursts in my eyes cleared, and I saw him standing threateningly over me, his manhood dangling low above my head, his arms raised, with his fists grasping his carved staff, ready to end my life with a single blow. But before he brought the cudgel down in a swift, killing blow, he looked intently down at me. I knew the expression of his face well. I had seen that look in the eyes of Graybeard and then the elder of the Gentle People—right before they joined with me. I knew then that, though he might kill me, it wouldn't be then, at that moment. And I watched has he slowly pulled his arms down and let the tip of the carved staff rest on the ground next to my shoulder.

Big Stick leaned down, picked me up, and slung me over his shoulder. I bounced painfully, belly against hard-muscled shoulder, as he trotted through the forest area and across the scrub fringe that none of the Gentle People had gone into and returned to tell of, and we were rising up the rocky slopes at the base of the cliffs and higher even by a narrow path cut in the rocks. In a short time we reached the yawning maw of a cave opening up behind a narrow ledge of rock looking out over the land toward the shining surface of the forbidden waters.

Big Stick carried me into the cave, where, off to the side, there lay a pallet of rushes covered by the fur of a teeth monster and where Big Stick rolled me off of his shoulder and onto my back on the soft, warm fur.

I was terrified. I could tell by the skins he covered the ground of the cave with that he was a hunter of the teeth monster—a successful hunter. And all of the Gentle People lived in fear of the unanswerable power and cruelty of the teeth monster, who attacked our clearings at will and carried off whomever it chose to feed on. How was I to protect myself against a Sharpspear who could sleep on the pelt of a teeth monster he had slain himself?

I couldn't. And thus, I put up no defense to what came next. In fact, this was little different than I knew under the power of the elders of the Gentle People.

After laying me on the fur, Big Stick went over to the edge of the cave and placed his carved cudgel on a rock ledge above my reach. He turned then and gave me a look that conveyed that I had better harbor no designs to reach the stick. I lowered my eyes demurely, hoping he would understand I would make no such attempt.

When I raised my eyes again, he was standing over me as I lay on my back on the fur pallet and looking down at me with hooded, lustful eyes that told me what he wanted. While I watched, he wrapped his hand around that gigantic poker of his and made it even larger and standing out from the bush of hair at the center of him. While he was doing this, he nudged the insides of my legs with his feet. I understood that he was demanding that I spread my legs for him. And in consideration of the size of his poker, he need not ask for that. I knew what was to come next, and I knew I wanted my legs spread as much as possible. I spread them, bent my knees and placed the soles of my feet on the fur pallet.

Big Stick came down on his knees between my legs on the pallet, and with rough hands, he grabbed me by the waist and dragged my hips up over his thighs, and the breeding began. Brutal, splitting, deep reaching, producing in me waves of pain and pleasure that I answered with writhing and crying out and moaning and groaning. The most giant tree of the forest, if forced up inside me, could not have filled and stretched and worried me as his poker, moving up inside me, did. And when his bush was joined with mine, he began to pump me and to mutter and grunt to himself and hum a tune of victory. All of which seemed to please Big Stick and spur him on to breed me not once, but three times before he was too spent to go on and rose from me, causing me to fall back onto the pallet.

I was totally taken and exhausted and spent and just lay there, arms akimbo, my legs too numb to even try to draw them together again. But still, he did not trust that I would not try to escape. He left my side briefly and went into a chamber of the cave behind this one and came back quickly with strips of animal hide, with which, while smiling at me, and cooing to me to convey who knows what point to me, he tied my wrists together. And then, as I groaned—and cried out when he grasped my wounded ankle—he brought my legs together and tied them off at the ankles.

He did, however, rummage around at the corner of the cave and come back with a poultice of wet leaves and herbs that he wrapped around my swollen ankle.

And then, as night was forcing the retreat of day, he moved out to the rock ledge at the cave entrance, and my eyes went wide as he created magic, calling down from the heavens the god of consuming heat, from which we Gentle People ran when brush went all angry hot and yellow and red in the middle of the periodic rumbling storm and died down to uselessness. He had the consuming heat god in front of him in the middle of the ledge, as he crouched down and held a dead and plucked bird over it on a sharp stick, watching as the bird sizzled and turned blackish.

Soon, Big Stick rose and brought the skewered bird over to me and pointed it at me. I whimpered and drew back from it—and from him—as best I could. He laughed then and put his mouth to the bird and sank his teeth into it and came away with a large chunk, which he then chewed noisily and swallowed.

I shrank away from him in horror and was almost sick. He indeed was one of the Meateaters—his smell alone as he was carrying me up into the cliffs and then again when he was breeding me had been enough to confirm this. But now there was no doubt.

He pushed the bird at my face again and muttered something guttural, which I took to mean he wanted me to slash at the bird myself with my teeth, but I just grimaced and turned onto my side, away from him.

I heard him laugh again, but now the laugh sounded more hollow, not so happy.

When night fell and the consuming heat god no longer proudly danced outside the cave entrance as before, Big Stick came back into the cave, unbound my ankles, and laid down beside me. He put his arms around me, and I could feel his hands gliding over my body. I relaxed, knowing he was going to have me again—and again and again and again, if that was what he wanted—and that there was nothing I could do about it but be glad that while he was breeding me, he wasn't taking my life from me. He was arousing me, taking me to the other side of my fear. And he knew he was pleasing me, because my own man thing betrayed my interest. We were both breathing heavily, and I was sighing my surrender. he laid a hand on my belly and pulled my hips back into his lap and my opening onto his hard penetrator.

This time when he bred me, I opened more quickly and willingly to his great tool working up inside me, and when the rhythm of his pumping started, my hips, almost involuntarily, moved to join him in the dance of the breeding. And when I moaned, he sighed. And when I sighed, I felt his lips on my body. And when I gave up my seed, he laughed a low, pleased laugh, and then I felt his seed flowing deep inside me.

The next morning, he untied me and took me out to a corner of the ledge and let me unburden myself. Then he carried me back into the cave chamber and tied me up again and, taking his staff down from the ledge, climbed down from the cave entrance to the forest floor below, and left me there.

For some time, I worked hard to free myself—and I finally succeeded. I then scrambled on hands and knees over toward the cave entrance and, bypassing the ring of the home of the consuming heat god, which was now all black and sending up wisps of smoke, I moved toward the edge of the ledge and peered down the steep incline of the narrow path leading to the flat scrub lands below. I had almost built up the courage to try to pull myself down the path and somehow hide in the scrub land until I felt able to move back into the forest in the night, when I saw them.

The two Meateaters from the previous day. The ones Big Stick had taken me from. They were moving up the trail, crouching and looking up. The lead one saw me peering over the edge, and he gave me a cruel smile and a deep-throated laugh.

I started clambering back toward the cave entrance, my mind racing on whether I had seen anywhere to hide or take a last stand in there, wondering if it would be folly to withdraw to the chamber beyond the chamber, when I was overtaken by a hand grabbing my injured ankle and, as I yelped in pain, flipping me onto my back just inside the cave entrance.

I looked up at the two Meateaters standing over me, grinning their nasty smiles, and I knew instantly from the hardness of their man things what they had in mind.

The fat one moved around me, went down on his knees, and reached for me with both hands. He was strong, and much bigger and more powerful than I was. He lifted me off the ground with his hands wrapped around my waist and turned me, facing away from him, looking into the sneering eyes of the other Meateater, and pulled my channel down on his fat taker. I cried out in pain and terror—and at the taking. He wasn't long, but his man thing was plump, and I was not prepared to receive him. I fought against him, but the struggling only lodged his penetrator more solidly inside me.

And then the other Meateater moved in toward me on his knees. He grabbed my hips with his hands and tilted my pelvis up toward him, and his hard man thing was entering me as well, on top of that of the other Meateater. His was longer than the first, and I gurgled and grunted my pain and frustration as he was the one who began to move his taker in and out of my channel. He hands went to my throat, and he was squeezing me there, and I was fighting for air, and seeing all of my ancestors pass before my eyes, knowing that this was my day.

But then it was the two Meateaters who where yelping in fear, and I saw the swinging of my Big Stick's carved cudgel, and the two Meateaters were being dragged away from me and beaten mercilessly.

As my eyes came into focus, I saw that Big Stick had returned and was fighting both of the other Meateaters—and mastering them with little effort at all with great swings of his staff, many of which were connecting. The two Meateaters were lucky to manage to scramble away from him and down the pathway from the rock ledge outside the cave entrance before he had brought his cudgel up for a killing blow.

I saw him struggle briefly in indecision. Whether to follow them down the path and dispatch them when he caught up to them or to check to see how I fared. Something inside me began to change toward him when I saw that he quickly chose to stay with me. I felt his hands glide over my body, feeling for damage. Having found none other than the red welts on my neck, he gently picked me up and returned me to the pallet.

He surely saw the bindings that I had managed to shed myself of, but he gave no indication of whether he thought I had escaped them myself or that this was the work of the two Meateaters. He must have decided on the latter, as he did not bind me again, perhaps thinking that I might have defended myself better if I hadn't been bound.

He laid me gently on the pallet, and I could see that his man thing wanted to breed again. I steeled myself for having him deep inside me again. But he didn't take me, and I surprised myself by feeling a pang of disappointment that he didn't. Instead, after laying his carved staff on the rock ledge, he went back to the mouth of the cave and returned with a reed basket full of an assortment of fruits and berries.

He offered these to me one by one. At first I was afraid he had picked this way to dispatch me, because some of the berries were poisonous. But when I separated the fruit and berries and frowned at the collection of those that were inedible, he seemed to understand. And he never brought those back to me again when he foraged for my food. And as I ate, he went back to the cave entrance and resummoned the consuming heat god and cooked his own meat over it.

All the time he ate, he watched me. His look was a tender one, but his penetrator remained hard, so I knew what he was thinking the whole time. He had brought me food that I could eat. He had saved me from the other Meateaters. And I knew now that I would not try to escape again. Down there, in the scrub lands, lurked those other Meateaters, all of whom wished me harm. I knew now that I would never feel safe away from Big Stick's sight. I knew this was not a safe or a hopeful situation either. But I had always lived by the next beat of my heart. There was nothing different in this.

And, so, when Big Stick rose and moved slowly to me, a question in his face, not sure how he would be received, I turned toward him and raised up on my knees, and when he reached me, I held my hands out to take his man thing and leaned forward and opened my lips over the tip of it and began slowly swallowing it. He moaned, his eyes full of surprise and wonder, I'm sure never having experienced this special ritual of breeding that the Gentle People had perfected.

But then, shortly after, when I laid back and opened my arms to him, his smile and the strength and heat of his entering of me, and the quickness, the first time, of his release of his seed,

25

told me that he thoroughly enjoyed this new form of breeding pleasure.

All seemed to be well—at least for a few cycles of day and night—but then there came a day when Big Stick started to act strangely, and I began to fear what was in the chamber beyond the first one in the cave.

There came a day when the fruits and berries Big Stick had brought me had been consumed. But when he took his carved cudgel down from the rock ledge and made to leave the cave to replenish our supplies, I began to tremble and cry. He seemed to understand that I didn't feel safe, and, having checked the poultice of leaves and herbs he'd wrapped around my ankle and determining that the swelling had gone almost completely down, he signaled that I could go with him.

He was very thoughtful and attentive, and we moved slowly, him supporting me with his strong arms when needed. His hands stayed on my body longer than necessary when he guided me, and I could see from his poker that he would willingly lay me down and breed me again at any excuse.

I found that was what I wanted now too, but I was afraid the ankle would last only so long and that we had better do our gathering as quickly as possible and get back to the cave before dark.

In addition to his carved staff, Big Stick had brought his spear, the magical one with the hard, gray tip on it that allowed him to bring down game with only a few tries. He did so with grace and power, and I admired the way he moved. I also began to wonder if the Gentle People too, would become Meateaters if we discovered the magic of the pointed stick. And the magic of controlling the god of the consuming heat too—and the power to bring down the teeth monster. There was no end to the wonder of the Sharpspears. And, when thinking of Big Stick, in particular, there was wonder too at the power of his man thing that made me moan for him when he moved inside me.

We gathered game for Big Stick and fruits and berries for me—and I showed Big Stick which were the edible nuts as well. He at least feigned interest in what I was showing him, and I glowed at the thought that he wanted to share with me. This was nothing like the land of the Others, where the only connections were in fighting over a big nut or joining one body with another briefly and furiously. Then, while we were in the forest, Big Stick moved into a dimly lit dell and pulled up some of the moss growing there and put it in the basket with the fruit. I tried to take it out again and to signal to him that it wasn't edible, but he became agitated, insisting that it remain, so remain it did.

I assumed we were ready to return to the cave then, but Big Stick didn't stop the hunt there. On our way back to the cave, he stopped along the base of the cliff. He was looking for something, but I didn't know what. But then he exclaimed in a happy sound, and I looked up on the face of the cliff. He was running his hands along seams of lumpy sandy dirt between the layers of the cliff rock. And when I looked at them, I saw that they were in different colors. Red, brown, and yellow.

Big Stick untied several hide pouches that had been hanging from his hide-strip belly belt and took the tip of his pointed spear and began to shave off this lumpy dirt into his pouches, one pouch for each different color of dirt.

I sat on my haunches and watched him in awe. Some more magic, I wondered.

And then I became more sure this had something to do with magic, but less sure whether it was good magic.

He seemed excited, keyed up, when we arrived back in the cave. Twilight was falling as we got there, and he almost absentmindedly settled me on the breeding pallet and pushed the baskets of fruits, berries, and nuts at me, letting me select my own.

He hurriedly summoned the consuming heat god and wolfed down a half-cooked small animal of the scrub lands.

Then he started the most strange of rituals, one that would go on for evenings to come. He usually came to me at this time of night and stood before me, as I paid homage to his poker with my lips and then lay down for him. But this evening after his meal he paid no attention to me at all. Instead, he took out his pouches of lumpy dirt and picked up a rock with an indented bowl shape in it. He sprinkled some of the dirt from one of the pouches into the depression in the rock. After that he took up the shoulder bone of a large animal he'd hunted. I had always thought this was a weapon, and I shrank from him when he took it up, ever mindful that my time was surely coming to an end at some point soon. But he didn't dispatch me. Rather, he went over to the mouth of the opening into the chamber behind this one and crouched down and began to beat the lumpy sand dirt in the rock bowl with the shoulder bone. He was looking at me and smiling and humming while he did so. And I was thinking how strange the rituals of the Sharpspear people were.

After he seemed satisfied with this part of the ritual, he rose, with the rock bowl in his hand, and went over to the side of the cave, where our drinking water trickled down the cave wall from a fissure overhead. There, he filled the bowl with water, and, smiling at me in passing, he took the bowl into the back chamber. He returned and repeated this ritual in other rock bowls with the other two pouches of dirt.

The third time he came back, he took up a big staff of wood, which briefly made me fear for my life once more. But, without looking at me, he held the head of the staff inside the consuming heat god, until the god flared up in anger. Then when the staff came out of the god's grasp, there were two gods, one on the rock ledge outside the entrance to the cave and the other lapping around the head of the staff.

The cave chamber now was alive with shimmering light. There were seams of sparkling color running through the walls of the cave and several places where water seeped down in small rivulets, and the glow from the angry god bounced around the wall and made it come alive.

I thought Big Stick would come to me then, but, although he did bend down to me in passing, holding the angry god-tipped staff over his head, instead of reaching for me, he put his hand in the fruit basket and brought out the patches of moss that he had insisted we bring back.

Then he took the staff and disappeared into the back chamber and I again was in near darkness, with only the consuming heat god at the entrance to the cave reflecting light back to me. I lay down, sadly, wondering what magic Big Stick was summoning forth, and worrying about myself—and, most strangely—worrying about Big Stick as well.

I slowly went to sleep, as did the consuming heat god at the cave entrance.

Sometime in the night, Big Stick did come to me and breed me. And he did so in a new excitement and exuberance I had not experienced from him before. Deep in the breeding, he pulled me up with him as he rose to his feet. I was connected to him at our pelvises, and I wrapped my legs around his thighs, under his big, firm buttocks, as he walked us out to the entrance of the cave, and he bred me deep and strongly as we both looked up at the twinkling dots of consuming heat gods in the night sky.

When he put me back down, he didn't come down to me to sleep, me in his embrace, as he had been doing at night before this strange ritual started. Rather he went back to the cave entrance and pulled several twigs, with blackened ends, out of the dying consuming heat god and carried them into the back chamber.

He did this for four days. And I was afraid that he had gone mad.

And the more I thought about it and the longer he did it the more sure I was that he had gone mad and that something terrible was happening back there in that forbidden chamber, something deadly. My worst fears were realized the night he came to me and I woke with the fingers of one of his hands before my face. They were dripping in a bloody-red fluid. I sat up and screamed, knowing my time had come.

Big Stick looked surprised and then concerned. And then when he saw the blood red dripping on his fingers, he laughed and wiped his fingers off on the teeth monster hide. Then he stood and picked me up in his arms and carried me toward the back chamber.

I cried and whimpered, not wanting this to be my day, not wanting now to leave him. Not knowing how I had displeased him. Beside myself in wanting another chance to please him and stay as we were before these four chilling days.

When he carried me into the back chamber, my eyes opened in wonder and awe. The staff tipped with the angry consuming heat god was wedged into the rock wall and was sending light reflecting all over a chamber slightly smaller than the one at the cave entrance but with much thicker veins of the sparkling earth between the white-gray rock.

That's not what caught my attention, though. The inside walls of the cave were covered with wondrous, colored scenes of animals and men in motion. Literally all of the walls were alive with action, depicting the lives of the Meateater Sharpspears. The paint—in rich reds, and browns, and yellow and defined by tracings in black—on the wall beside the lighted staff, however, was still wet.

Big Stick set me down on the rock floor of the cave, and I slowly approached this obviously still-unfolding scene. I knew now what all of the ritual was about. Big Stick was creating a scene on the walls of this inner sanctum. And not just any scene. He was a master depicter. I could clearly see that he was painting our life together from the scene of his having taken me—saving me, I now knew—to our first breeding and the attack of the two Meateaters and his learning of what I could eat and our trip to the outside world for our food—and for the colors he was painting with. And I could see now, looking down at the lumps of moss with paint on them, for the brushes. The twigs with the blackened ends were there, obviously used for the outlining.

And, in the last frame, still being painted, appeared the gigantically big Meateater Sharpspear and the small man of the Gentle People—joined as one contentment on their faces. He had the smiles on the faces of both outlined with the charcoal but not yet colored in.

I saw that there was another fur-covered pallet in this room, and I turned and pressed on Big Stick's chest until he realized that I wanted him to lie on the pallet on his back. He smiled as he laid down. I didn't have to prepare either his or my penetrators—I had realized days ago that we needed only be in close proximity to both be ready for the breeding. And then I mounted his man thing with my channel and rode him into paradise, my eyes feasting on the magnificence of his wall paintings and wondering what this new, strange, happy feeling of belonging and wanting meant. But knowing without a doubt that the feeling was one I wanted to keep and that it all centered on this big man I was filled with—my Big Stick.

Chapter Three: Early Time

I stuck to my resolve never to venture alone outside the cave. My resolve, however, crumbled into a million pieces—and not because of anything I could have helped. One time Big Stick left the cave to forage for food, and he did not come back. We already needed food badly when he left. He waited until he could wait no longer, saying that he did not want to leave me but could not take me with him—that there was disturbance upon the air in the land of the Sharpspears. That bands of the Yellow People had been coming into the land and that there was war upon our world.

But at last he had to go—and because of the danger abroad, he refused to take me with him.

And then he didn't return.

When I could bear the hunger—and, yes, the sense of worry and even grief—no longer, I left the cave myself and descended the cliff face into the forest below. I cannot say that I cared whether I lived or died at that point, but my hunger had overpowered my willingness to starve myself to death in mourning for my lost Big Stick.

I immediately fell into trouble. I no sooner than started off in the forest then I heard thrashing about in the forest. They came close enough that I could smell them. Meateaters. A band of Sharpspears. I moved away from them—only to come close to another band of them. Turning again and then a third time—helped by my hunger—made me disoriented.

I kept moving. I did manage to find food and water, but then I heard a band of warriors nearby again—very close—and I just turned and stole away. I walked and walked, without knowing where I was going. When I eventually came to a clearing, I saw that I had moved very close to the land that rose up sharply to meet the sky.

I heard voices, but they weren't the primitive grunts of the Sharpspears. It was some sort of language—some means of verbal communication—but it wasn't the language of the Gentle People either. It was more complex, and it was spoken in differing tones, almost sing song. Strangely, though, it was harsh as well as sing song. Curiosity got the best of me, and I stealthily moved across the clearing to a fringe of trees on the other side. The forest wasn't dense here, though. There was another clearing beyond—a strange clearing, as it was really like a path, but much wider than ones the Gentle People made between their village and field.

And when I got to where I could see who was making the harsh sing-song utterances, I was amazed—and numb in shock. There was some sort of wooden contrivance on the cleared path. It had round circles of wood at its corners that raised its platform off the ground. At the near end of this contrivance was a long wood stick that curved up. A strange-looking man—yellow skinned and slanty eyed, with a dirty loin cloth around his middle, was standing this side of the contrivance. He had a wooden yoke around his neck and his wrists were bound to the end of this on both sides. There was another yoke beside him, but it was on the ground. Tied to it and also lying on the ground was another man such as the first. A third man, covered in a white cloth, also yellow skinned and slanty eyed, was standing beside these two and was beating the man on the ground with a whip.

I should have turned and fled. But even if I had, I would have run into the small party of other yellow-skinned, slanty-eyed men covered in white clothes who were stealing in behind me.

As, yoked to the wagon and straining along with the other man to pull the contrivance up the side of the land reaching for the sky, I tried to think on what was happening to me and why I was here, I chose to think that it didn't matter. Big Stick had not come back. I had willed myself to be no more. The pain and strain of pulling this contrivance—and knowing that another man had died in this yoke before me—spelled my fate well enough.

On the other side of the mountain, I was astonished to find new wonders I'd never seen before. The Yellow People sheltered not in the forest under branches, nor in a cave, nor even in the grass piles of the Gentle People. Their shelters were made of wood and were squared off in neat four-sided bundles.

I didn't live in one of these shelters, though. And the only times I went in one was when the man with the whip pulled me into one and slapped my thighs open and made groaning sport of my hole with his penetrator—which gave me no problem, being much smaller than that of Big Stick.

Where I was sheltered was under a tree, tied by leather strippings to the trunk of the tree. There weren't even low branches for me to hide from the elements under. Whereas the Yellow People lived in wooden shelters—and had mastered the leaping, hot flickering fingers that warmed within rock containers inside these wooden shelters—I was sheltered no better than I had been when living among the Others. Much worse.

For untold changes of light to dark and back to light, when I was nudged away in the dark, I would be handed a bowl of gruel with sticky grains of white in it. Happily, no one of the Yellow People tried to make me eat meat, although they themselves ate fish from the waters. Then, before light returned, I was herded with others, some Yellow People, some Sharpspears, but all as enslaved as I was, out into a water-covered field, where I soon learned along with the others how to work with growing and dividing and cultivating the white sticky grains that I was given to eat. They were filling, though, so I could not be sad about that.

During my time with the Yellow People, I was slowly able to begin to understand that the sounds they made had meanings and to learn what some of these meanings were. I never, however, was able to make those sounds myself. There were just too many of them and they were too complex—and the Yellow People sang them just too quickly. I marveled, though, that these people not only had fields of food plants they laid out nearly like those of the Gentle People, but also that they had wooden shelters for themselves and conveyances that moved over the ground and a way to communicate many thoughts and meanings to each other.

As the world became cooler again in another cycle, the water was drained from the field and we harvested the grains, which were put in tightly woven baskets and loaded onto the contrivance with the four wooded circles at the corner.

Then, once again, I found myself bound to the yoke of this conveyance—for that was what it was, a land vessel to carry the baskets of sticky white grains—and I was helping to pull the conveyance back up the side of the land reaching for the sky. This was only slightly less backbreaking than trying to keep the conveyance from running over and crushing me on the way back down the other side.

We seemed to be moving on the same wide path where I had first encountered the Yellow People, and pushing toward the ribbon of sand that ran into the broad sea stretching to the horizon where the first light after the dark rose in an eye-torturing disk.

We were struggling along, with the man with the whip jabbering harsh sounds at us and flicking us when we weren't moving fast enough, when he stopped jabbering in a gurgling sound. I looked around in time to see him crumple to the ground with a pointed stick running completely through his chest and out his backside.

Sticks were flying all around us, and the other Yellow People who had been walking around the line of conveyances others like me were pulling began falling down or turning this way and that with their own pointed stakes at the defensive.

I have no idea how long this went on, because I felt a stinging pain in my shoulder and looked down in surprise to find that I too had been struck through with a pointed stick. I went down like a rock, with my last sensation being of rolling down between the two circles of wood at the front of the conveyance I had been pulling.

When I woke, I was feverish and sensed that I was jabbering in some variation of the Yellow People's language. My arm, which was covered in leaves felt like it was too hot for me to bear, and my eyes could not focus.

Through I cloud, I saw a huge body of a male leaning over me, lifting my head and pouring water into my mouth from a soaked piece of white cloth. Nonsensically I had the vision of the white cloth being just like that which covered the Yellow People. Only later, when I was more aware, did I find out that this was exactly what it was.

I knew that the man giving me the water was a Meateater Sharpspear. As a habit, this realization caused me to painfully open my thighs, ready to receive him. That could be the only purpose for him trying to revive me.

Later—I know not how long ago later—I opened my eyes gain. The fever was gone, and my vision was clear—or at least not nearly as cloudy as it had been before. I saw that I was in a cave and I was alone, although I heard grunting and humming sounds coming from the dark recesses of the cave.

I dragged myself to a sitting position and winced at the pain in my shoulder. But I saw that the leaves were the right ones—the ones that would pull any poison from the pointed stick out of me and would help heal the wound.

I was in pain, but it was not too bad. And the pain told me that I was alive. That in itself was a surprise—whether a good surprise or a bad one I did not know.

I managed to get up on my feet. I would have moved better on all fours, except that the pain was less on my shoulder when I stood. There was a thick stick near the mat I was on and I used it as a crutch.

I moved slowly, but deliberately, toward the back of the cave, toward where I heard the sounds of a man coming from. I could see that it would be no use moving toward the mouth of the cave. Its floor was not at ground level. Beyond the ledged outside the cave, I could see the tops of trees. I would never escape that way.

And I was tired, so tired. I had no idea what new dangers and difficulties faced me now, but I decided that I would face them—that I would find this Sharpspear and lie under him—and then maybe he would let me go, go to another world. Surely whatever world there was out there after this one, it would be less cruel to me than how I had existed to now.

When I got to the back of this chamber of the cave, I saw that there was another chamber beyond it. And that the second chamber was filled with the light from the dancing orange and red miracle that some of the worlds I had lived in seemed to know how to make—but that my own world of the Others did not.

The Sharpspear was crouching, facing the wall of the cave. The wall was covered in colorful drawings—drawings that started to flood back into my memory as both my mind and eyes cleared.

Big Stick was painting on the wall. A new episode to our story. The story of my return to the cave. And to him.

He turned and looked at me and opened his arms wide. I looked down at the stick I was leaning on. It was Big Stick's carved cudgel.

Chapter Four: Present Time

"I tell you I did not undermine you in the acquisition of those stone carvings. I would never do anything like—"

"Gloria told me, Timothy. She told me that you revealed our bid to the Houston Museum so that they could underbid us."

"Gloria is a bitch, Jay. If anyone did it, she did. You know she's been trying to break us up. I think she has eyes for you herself."

"Here, give me a leg up. I looks like a cave entrance up there. And I don't know. I just don't know. I thought you cared."

"You don't know how much I care. I'm here with you now, aren't I. This wasn't the wisest place to be—and I told you so. There are still headhunters around here. One of the Rockefeller boys disappeared near here, you know. They never found him. And Amelia Earhart."

"Shut up, Timothy, and give me that boost."

The two men made their way up to the ledge in front of the cave door.

"Would you look at this?" Timothy said in awe, as they entered the cavern. "This might go back to earliest times. There definitely was habitation here. Look, they had fires out there on the ledge outside the opening. They knew about fire."

"There appears to be another chamber behind this one, Timothy. Come, bring the flashlights. I want to see if there's something—"

"Holy-moly, would ya look at that—?"

The two of them stood there, in awe, for several minutes. They trained the beam of the light back and forth over the wall of the second chamber. There were cave drawings—and in color, in whites and yellows and browns and reds all across the back wall. They had difficulty determining where it started and where it ended—assuming there was any progression there at all.

"It's magnificent," Jay uttered when he could speak.

"I haven't seen anything like this outside of the caverns of France—maybe not even there," Timothy answered in a voice laced with wonder.

Trained scientists that they were, the two moved to find the beginning, once they recognized that it, indeed, was a continuing story.

It was thirsty work, and Timothy went back to the main cave to retrieve their water canteens.

"It's a love story," Jay called out at length, having followed the progression along the wall. "It's obviously the life of two men devoted to each other. And it lasted to the death. Here, at the end, the smaller of the men crouched over the larger one. Unmistakably tears falling on the dead lover. And this last panel in a decidedly different hand than the rest of it. And, oh my god, come back in here, Timothy. I think there are a couple of skeletons back here."

Jay stood and turned. Timothy was standing at the entrance of the second chamber. He had a strange expression on his face and his arms were half raised, cradling an object. Jay looked closely and saw that it was a staff—a cudgel, really— intricately carved and notched.

"I found this on a high rock ledge in the other room."

"Quite a find," Jay said. "The museum will love it. You'll no doubt get the assistant curator position you've wanted now. It must be eons old."

"I want you to have it. This will be your find. I didn't undermine your acquisition of the rock painting that went to the

Houston. And I want you to believe me by my giving this to you. You will rise to curator on this."

"Put it down, Timothy."

"Why?"

"Look into my eyes, Timothy. You'll know why then. The love story on this wall is deeply affecting and suggestive. I believe you and I apologize for doubting you—and I am in the mood."

"Here? Now?"

"And why not? This seems to have been the perfect love nest. The walls do not lie."

Labyrinth

Chapter One: Phitio to Brixia

"Come now, I know there must be a price." The general placed his wine cup on the taboret next to the marble bench and looked scoffingly at the governor seated on the other bench. Both were looking out into the grassed courtyard, where the beautiful young and small blond man was reclining on the lip of a fountain, his back leaning on a gargoyle spouting water, and strumming a lute. The young man was naked except for a stark-white loin cloth and sandals that rose in criss-crossed leather straps up his finely sculpted calves as he was taking in the sun's rays. The whiteness of the cloth emphasized the deep tan of his lithe torso and legs. From where the two leaders were sitting, it looked like the sun's rays radiated from his perfectly formed body and lit up the whole world. Off on the other side of the courtyard sat a middle-aged woman of both regal and attentive bearing, who was clearly keeping a watchful eye on the young man and a vigilant eye on the general and the governor as well.

"It isn't as easy to shop for a prince as for a serving man," the governor murmured. "Young Nyke there is an institution—a near god—in the land of Phitio. He is here for safety because the main island of Phitio is under siege from the Cenopolis forces. I am sure he would be highly decorative at your court in Brixia, but Nyke is not just the crown prince's brother, he is our golden priest as well. He serves a function in the ceremonial succession in Phitio, and as the king's time seems near, Nyke must be preserved to that day at all costs."

"It is for nothing ceremonial that I want the lad," said General Lykaois. And as he did so, he parted his robe to show the governor a manly, fully engorged cock curving up from his lower belly. "You know what I want of him. You guarantee he is a virgin?"

"Yes, of course he is still a virgin. That too is decreed in our customs. But, please, you must cover yourself, General. By all means don't let the harridan over there see you exposed thus for the young man. That is the young prince's mother, the second queen, although she continually declares she is first queen and that the mother of the crown prince has hidden the time of her own birthing so that her son will be recognized as in ascendance. You simply cannot understand how delicate these matters are in Phitio at this time—none of which is helped by being under siege by Cenopolis. Perhaps we need to turn to the discussions that brought your delegation here, General—discussions on what Brixia can do to help turn back—or, better yet, defeat—the forces of Cenopolis."

"You intrigue me," Lykaois said, ignoring the governor's attempt to turn the conversation. "What is it about this young prince that makes you reticent about giving me access—for a price? You have said the prince is still a virgin. That's hard to believe, given his apparent age and his beauty, and having been given into your hands. I saw you debauch two young lads last evening. For the price I offer, I would gladly let you watch me greet and broaden that tender young hole. You enjoyed watching me render that small Nubian unconscious last evening."

"Prince Nyke is the Golden Priest. He must be at the king's burial ceremony as a virgin."

Lykaois gave the governor a gaze of noncomprehension.

"It is how we solidify our succession in Phitio. There are only two recognized sons of the king—the crown prince and the second son, Prince Nyke, although there is an undercurrent of support for Prince Nyke as the first son. To maintain loyalty and cut off any possibility of disunity in our multi-island nation, when the crown prince attends his inauguration as king, he must stand alone in the succession."

"You mean?—"

"Yes, the ceremony of succession includes the sacrifice of all Golden Priests. And they depart this life as virgins—known neither by woman nor man. That keeps the succession pure and the possibility of bastard sons here and about unlikely. And now, shall we move into the palace and begin our talks on the mutual benefit of neutralizing Cenopolis?"

"Not until we talk about the price for Prince Nyke. I know you must have your price, and I know you are clever enough to find the way. If you are just going to waste luscious sweet meat like that, who needs to know whether he went to his death a virgin or not? And, as for toying with me in this, you'll find that I'm not just an emissary of Brixia. I *am* Brixia."

"Come, my randy general," the governor said with a smile and a small laugh that showed a bit of the strain he was under. "Perhaps you would like to enjoy a brief respite before we speak of anything further. Here, what do you think of young Paulo here? Do you not fancy golden-red curls? He's as young as Nyke and also a virgin. He only entered service at the palace yesterday straight from the Temple of Virgins. He is untouched, I swear."

The governor was looking at the visiting general, co-ruler of Brixia, with anxiety. He had brought in Paulo, a temple virgin, to use in the negotiations with general. He hadn't anticipated Lykaois having seen Prince Nyke, though. He had other instructions on Nyke, although he hadn't devised his plans yet. The crown prince, already acting for his quickly sinking father king, had burdened the governor of this remote island, one of the collection of islands merged as the State of Phitio, with too many responsibilities at once. There already was the matter of Nyke, and now, on top of that, the negotiations had developed with Brixia to come to Phitio's aid against the forces of Cenopolis, now investing the main island. And the Brixian general had already overplayed the intelligence on his interests and capacities. The governor would be hard pressed to provide

41

the next virginal youth after Paulo had been spent. If, indeed, the governor even could turn the general's attention away from Nyke.

General Lykaois was gazing out into the courtyard again now, drinking in the luscious body of Prince Nyke, as the young man stretched out and yawned and lightly rubbed his hard belly, seemingly entirely unaware he was being watched.

As they both watched Nyke, the governor maneuvered the somewhat reluctant small-bodied Paulo around to close beside the bench where the general lounged. Paulo was wearing nothing but a loincloth that covered his privates but fully exposed his pert buttock cheeks, and it was upon one of his buttocks that the governor maneuvered the general's hand.

Prince Nyke adjusted his position on the fountain ledge, raising one leg, knee bent and heel on fountain edge, while the other grabbed for the grassy ground at a wide angle. The general moaned quietly as he realized that the loin cloth had folded away and he could see the golden fuzz on the young prince's balls. The prince's mother gave a sharp look at where the general and the governor were sitting, but other than pursing her lips, she made no utterance or movement.

The next moan came from the young Paulo, as the Brixian general, while keeping his eyes riveted on the lounging prince, had unconsciously palmed the young red-headed servant's buttocks cheek and entered the young man's virginal passage with a thick finger. Paulo clutched tightly onto the general's silver breastplate and whimpered and groaned as the general began to absentmindedly finger fuck him.

The governor leaned his lips down to the general's ear and whispered, "If you fuck the young servant right here, the harridan over there will fly with her young charge. Do come into the palace proper for a dalliance and a short nap and then we will refresh ourselves and begin our talks of mutual defense."

About all the general heard was the suggestion that his real quarry might fly, and so he stood and permitted the governor to guide him—and the young Paulo—toward an interior door. Lykaios' two bulky bodyguards had been standing at loose attention at the door they approached, and after, first Lykaios, and then the governor passed through, each guard took

Paulo by an arm and lifted his body off the ground and followed along behind the two officials.

Lykaios loosened his robes as they entered the bedchamber he had been given and they fell away from his body, revealing that he had maintained the thick, hard cock he had uncovered earlier. He reached around and dug a fist into Paulo's golden-red curls, as the two bodyguards released the young man and he started falling to the floor, and dragged the young man across the marble floor on his knees and slammed him down on his belly on the elevated end of a dining couch.

Paulo was gasping and groaning at the rough treatment. Lykaios tore his loin cloth from him, positioned his cock head at the tiny entrance of Paulo's channel and started to work his way inside. Paulo's screams of pain and invasion were stifled as Lykaios stuffed the loin cloth in his mouth, grabbed the young man's waist, and concentrated on getting his cock inside the tight passage. Paulo was reaching down along the line of the dining couch, trying to gain a hold on the leather covering. He lifted his head and screamed through the loin cloth gag, as Lykaios grabbed his ankles in beefy fists, pulled his legs wide, struck home, deep, with his cock, and began to fuck Paulo's channel in long, deep strokes.

Satisfied that Lykaios's attention had been diverted, the governor left the chamber and went back to his office, where his steward—the only one he confided in—was waiting for him.

"How are the negotiations going?" the steward asked quietly, putting his lips near the ear of his seated master to discourage the listening walls.

"It isn't going at all. The oversexed general has seen Nyke and is in full rut for him. I should have kept them separate. The general is determined to buy and deflower the prince. The barbarian. All of those landed states are homes for barbarians."

The governor was especially piqued, because he had planned to have the servant Paulo for his own tonight—and now it was quite evident that the young man would be ruined.

The steward looked thoughtful and then he lowered his lips again and said, "Perhaps . . . perhaps, master, this is an opportunity. Perhaps you can devise a way through this to meet the demands of the crown prince as well as conclude a treaty with Brixia."

"And what sort of plan would that be?" the governor asked in exasperation, but his eyes widened and then slitted and a slight smile came across his face, as the steward started whispering in his ear once more.

It was with a secret little smile on his face that the governor returned to General Lykaios' bedchamber, assuming that the general might be thirsty or hungry after his taking of Paulo and might wish some light refreshment before retiring for an hour's rest. What he found, though, was that the general was far from tired of Paulo's body, so he sat on the dining couch the two had been using when he left and stole his hand into the folds of his robes to enjoy the action.

Lykaios had taken Paulo to the bed and spread-eagled him on his back. His four extremities were spread taut and tied off with leather strappings at the four bedposts. His mouth was muffled now not by the loin cloth but by the general's cock, as the general straddled the young man's chest and leaned over him and used the leverage of his knees to face fuck the gurgling, gagging young man.

As the governor watched, Lykaios untied the young man's ankles, jack knifed Paulo's leg above his head, crouched over the young man's folded body, with his buttocks facing the young man's face, and started jack hammering down into Paulo's hole with his cock. Paulo was left free to scream his taking now, and the marble walls of the palace reverberated with his cries, which started at a high, loud pitch, but that diminished over time as he weakened and gained some pleasure from the taking.

When Lykaios had come, he climbed down from the bed and motioned to the two bodyguards.

"You may have what's left. Don't make a mess. Our host will think we are untidy and ungrateful."

Lykaios strode over to the governor while he pulled his robes back on and the governor, standing, moved to straighten his own garments. The governor looked beyond the Brixian general, his hope fading at any chance of enjoying Paulo tonight himself, as he watched the two burly bodyguards pull off the loin cloths under their battle skirtings and, still standing with their upcurled hard cocks dueling with each other, pick Paulo up and settle him between them. He somehow found the energy to cry out a bit more as the two giants worked their cocks in alongside each other in his now impossibly stretched hole. But by the time they were raising and lowering his channel on fully encased cocks, he was doing no more than moaning and whimpering softly and his limbs had lost all power, They just flopped back and forth between the rhythmically working bodies of the two meaty bodyguards.

"I wanted to check on whether you wanted some refreshment before you rested," the governor murmured, trying to keep his eyes off the cocking of his young servant, but unable to do so.

"No need for that," General Lykaois said, with a smile. "I am rejuvenated now and looking forward to our talks . . . eventually."

"Eventually?" the governor asked.

"Yes. We will not talk about mutual defense possibilities between Brixia and Phitio until we have settled on a price for Prince Nyke."

"You are a persistent man," the governor said with a slight frown.

"I have survived by concentrating on what I want," the general said. "Do you wish to have Brixia's might behind you in your defense against Cenopolis, or are you too unskilled in the arts of guile to work this out. I only wish to be the first one inside the prince. I won't ruin him to the point that anyone could—after a few days—discern that he had been deflowered. It will not be in either your or his interest to tell. And he is going to be sacrificed anyway."

The governor looked past the general at the tableau of three across the chamber. Paulo was now unconscious. Still the two men thrust their hips in rhythm, mining the young man's depths in consort.

General Lykaois looked in the direction too. "You needn't worry. That is a servant. I would not let my bodyguards touch a prince. All I want to do is widen his channel for him. He will thank me. Otherwise he will never have known that passion."

45

"You drive a hard bargain," the governor said, trying to effect a slight whine. "We shall see what can be done." Upon saying that, he turned his eyes away so that the general could not see the smile that he could not erase from his face.

* * * *

"I think that went well, my son." Phitio's second queen rose and moved out to the fountain area as soon as the governor and the Brixian general had moved off.

"He is a bigger brute than I thought he'd be, mother," Prince Nyke said. "And can we move into the shadows now. I think I will burn to a cinder. I thought they never would move away."

"He is what he needs to be," the queen said with a sigh. "He is a man who thinks and is led around by his phallus."

"And did you see it? He was showing it. He is a bull, mother. I don't think—"

"Yes, it is true we will need to make adjustments. Disgusting it was. As are all men's—except for you, my golden child," the queen said, her voice softening as she helped her son climb down from the rim of the fountain and they walked toward their own quarters.

"It is highly risky, this plan of yours, mother. And I fear it has little chance of success."

"All of life for those of us with royal blood is a labyrinth, Nyke. We are thrust in the maze by our birth and status, and we spend our lives twisting and turning, seeking the magic center, but even there, the labyrinth becomes a living thing—scheming and fighting against us and changing its avenues, its walls closing in on us. All we can do is continue to seek out the center and to survive for as long as possible."

"But do you think I really can cajole him to take me with him to Brixia? And where will you go, if I can?"

"If anyone can weave a spell around that man, it is you, Nyke. I saw how he watched you. I saw the flash of his horn, the hardness of it just from looking upon you. I think you will win him if only because you must. We are but two steps ahead of the crown prince and his schemes. You are too much of a threat to

46

him. He knows we have considerable support for you being the elder. He won't wait for the succession ceremony. He will do what he can to eliminate you earlier. That's why he agreed to your coming here, to the most remote island of the state. It wasn't to keep you safe from the sieging Cenopolis forces; it was to have you in a remote area so that the public will not see you being eliminated. Escaping to the land of Brixia and laying low until we can champion your cause at the death of the king is our—your—only hope. And it's what I have worked for."

"But you must live too, mother. If you die, all hope of forces coming to my support at the right time will evaporate."

"I will go to the island of Ia, if I can. It is where I come from, where my strength is. They will protect me from the crown prince's reach. In any event, he has his hands full with Cenopolis. But, come now, son. Come to our chambers. You must have a massage; I know your muscles ache from posing for the Brixian general for so long. And we must see about other adjustments too."

The queen sat there, by the marble table that Prince Nyke was stretched out on, admiring her perfectly formed golden child, as the Nubian slave worked the prince's limbs until he almost was nodding off to a sighing sleep.

Then, the prince lying on his back, the queen signaled and the Nubian slave picked up a crystal cylinder.

"No, not that one," the queen said. "We must make adjustments. That one there, two sizes larger than the one we have been using."

She watched, licking her lips slightly and with a secret little smile, as the Nubian slave slathered the cylinder in a greasy lotion. She leaned forward, giving the activity her full attention and Prince Nyke began to moan and groan softly, roll his hips slightly, and raise his pelvis and stroke the toweling under him with his rising cock, as the Nubian worked the greased cylinder into the prince's channel and started to turn it and stroke it ever deeper inside.

It was quite fortuitous, the queen was thinking, that she had had that glimpse of the Brixian general's monster of a phallus. Otherwise, her precious prince may not have been properly prepared for him.

* * * *

"You just sit here on this bench, sire, and we shall see if any of the players will find you. They have less time than will make you bored with waiting, and they will be eager to find you as I have set this gemstone as the prize for the one who does." The governor held up a large ruby, nearly the size of a sparrow's egg, to where it caught the reflection of the sun. "If none do find you, though, the gemstone is yours. I will come back for you when the time is up if you have not been discovered."

The governor had led Prince Nyke to the center of a vast boxwood maze in a corner of the gardens of the governor's palace. As the prince was led into the maze, the visiting Brixian general, Lykaois, and two nobles of the court that had come to the island with Nyke and the Second Queen were discussing forming up in hunt teams. When the governor came back out of the maze, he instructed each of General Lykaios's bodyguards to team with one of the prince's nobles and he declared that he himself would team with General Lykaois but would not, of course, give the general clues, because the governor knew how to get to the center of his maze.

Neither the two nobles nor the Second Queen, who was standing by, believed for a moment, of course, that the governor wouldn't be coaching the general. And there was no reason for them to expect fair play. This was an entertainment for the visiting general, with whom the governor had concluded a highly favorable friendship treaty the previous afternoon. Everyone present knew exactly who would win the game.

At this point, the governor took the egg-shaped ruby from the folds of his robe and lifted it up and said, "This is the prize for finding the young prince in the maze."

Nearly all present gasped at the beauty and size of the stone. The Second Queen alone reacted in anger. "Where did you get that ruby, governor?" she hissed. "It is not yours to give."

"No, your lady, it is not. Our visiting dignitary, General Lykaios, has generously supplied the prize. It is one worthy of your son, is it not, my queen?"

"It is worthy for a king, and my son is worthy to be a king," the Second Queen blurted out. For indeed she knew the ruby was worthy for a king, as it was a gem known as the King's Ruby, which had once been the treasury of her husband, the king of Phitio, and had been revered for the properties of good fortune that had been attached to it. It had disappeared from the treasury many years ago, its disappearance a mystery to all, although she had thought that her husband had taken the loss lightly at the time. At the time he was besotted with a captive youth who had been brought to court as a safeguard to a shaky armistice with a nearby state.

She was about to say something, but then her eyes turned to General Lykaios and narrowed, seeing him fully for the first time. Yes, she thought, he was very like that youth who had been brought to court and who had enchanted her husband, the king, so fully with his willingness and ability to take the king's cock that a treaty highly favorable to Brixia had eventually been penned and the youth had been sent home buried under love presents. It was all coming into place now; the ruby obviously had been one of those love presents. She set her mind to scheming to get the ruby back, but her thoughts were interrupted when she realized a voice was seeking her attendance.

"I am sorry there are no benches out here, your majesty," the governor said to the queen, even though until this morning there had been such. "Are you sure you wish to stand and wait for the game to proceed? There will be nothing to see, of course, and the day is hot."

"Certainly not, thank you, Governor," the queen answered with haughty tones. "I have no interest in boy's games. I will retreat to my chambers."

But it was not to her chambers that the queen retreated. Entering the palace, she hurried to her chambers where her retinue was all gathered and, as quietly and unobtrusively as possible, they all made their way to the harbor to board the queen's two royal sailing vessels. The two noblemen traversing the maze in the governor's game knew the risks they faced. If they made it to the vessels in time, they too would be sailing. If not, they would be staying to face the ire of the governor—and, by extension, that of the crown prince.

Meanwhile, as the three teams entered the maze, the two noblemen looked for clues on which avenue they were not to take. At signals from the governor from behind the Brixian general's back, one nobleman and Brixian bodyguard took a turn to the right and the other continued straight on the path while General Lykaios, following the governor's gesture with a smile, instinctively turned to the left.

It didn't take Lykaios very long to find the prince. It took the two Brixian bodyguards nearly double that time to dispatch their Phitio team members and to find the center of the maze, even though the governor had given them detailed instructions the night previously on how to reach it.

When they came upon the center of the maze, Lykaios was on his knees in front of the young prince and wooing him gently with talk of the young man's beauty. The governor was standing off to the side. Lykaios's men at his side now, he instructed one to put the governor to the sword, while he told the other to circle behind the prince and pin his arms. The governor, surprised by the duplicity, turned and started to run back into the maze. Even though he was in shock, he was quick enough to know that if he could get one turning between him and the bodyguard, he should be safe. But he didn't get that turning. When he had been run through, the bodyguard returned to the center of the maze in time to take one of Prince Nyke's legs and spread it up and out, as General Lykaios, his robes discarded and Prince Nyke's robes torn from his body, grasped the prince's other leg and worked his pelvis between the prince's thighs.

Prince Nyke was struggling. He was trying to make the best of looking shocked and betrayed and undone—and regally displeasured—but it was only partially shock—he also was in fear now. This was taking a turn for the violent that neither he nor his queenly mother had anticipated, and the prince genuinely feared for his life, being afraid that the general just meant to debauch him and then put him to the sword as had been done with the governor. The ruthless dispatching of the governor was something that had not been foreseen.

The general seemed to enjoy the prince's struggle, and he took a moment to pinch and prod with his hands and explore with his lips and teeth before he positioned his giant phallus at the rim of what he believed to be a virginal entrance and prepared to sheath himself between the young prince's glorious, golden-down-covered thighs.

But at that moment a shout went up that resounded through the palace halls and gardens. A warning was being trumpeted that forces of the Cenopolis were approaching the palace from across the land from the other side of the island. This was completely unexpected. All of the forces of Cenopolis had been assumed to be investing the central island and to be striking at the heart of the Phitio state. No one had anticipated that they would send auxiliary forces to subdue the separate little islands of the archipelago.

Surprised and worried now about his own safety, General Lykaios pulled away from Prince Nyke and wrapped his robes about his body. He signaled to his bodyguards, who seized the prince between them, and the small group stole posthaste to the harbor to their own flotilla of ships. They pushed off none too soon, as, with the governor dead, there was no one to form up the defenses of the palace, and the forces of the Cenopolis cut through the palace guards like they were butter and moved toward the harbor.

Once on board, the bodyguards were directed to take Prince Nyke to his cabin and leave him bound. Lykaios's ships had cleared the harbor when a shout went up that two vessels of the Phitio were also sailing and headed in their direction.

"Turn the ships to prepare for an attack from Phitio," Lykaios commanded the ship's captain. "They apparently aren't prepared to give up their prince without a fight."

"No need, I think," the captain answered. "Those ships have turned. I think they are fleeing the harbor just as we did. Just some Phitio nobleman abandoning their doomed island, as much on the wing as we are."

The general stood there, attentively and not fully convinced, until it was indeed obvious that the Second Queen's vessels were turning away from his ships' course and heading up the spine of the Phitio archipelago.

When the general was convinced that there was no pursuit, he turned and made his way down to his cabin. He pushed open the double doors to his commodious private cabin, its wooden walls painted a rich dark red, the decking covered with richly patterned carpets from the distant Orient, and a large mahogany desk with leather chairs gathered around. A large, four-poster bed with thick padding and covered with exotic animal skins was pushed against the bulkhead at the corner of the room. The far wall was taken up with diamond-paned windows set into the fantail of the vessel. The two bodyguards the general had taken to the island stood on either side of the door just inside the chamber. Prince Nyke, his upper arms bound tightly behind him and his ankles bound together was lying, naked on the bed.

The general motioned his dismissal with his hands and the two bodyguards moved through the doors and closed them in their wake.

The general stripped off his robes and went over to the corner of the cabin, where warm water nearly filled a copper tub. He took up a sponge and cleansed his body. Toweling himself off, he moved slowly over to the bed and sat down on the bed beside the bound prince. He ran his hand over the prince's torso, and Nyke shuddered in response, giving the general a wide-eyed, frightened look.

"The governor told me you were a virgin. Did he lie about that?"

"I have known no man or woman," the prince answered with a whisper. He saw no need to note that a cock need not be manned. He was trembling, as the general had taken his cock in his hand and was gently stroking it. This wasn't what Nyke had expected after the brutality of the attack in the maze.

The general was making little circles with the fingers of his other hand around Nyke's nipples and Nyke was moaning softly in response.

"We are on the high seas now," the general murmured. "There is no one to save or protect you here. And I will have you. You know that, don't you?"

"Yes," Prince Nyke whispered.

"I can either take you hard, or, if you let me have you without a struggle, I can release you from your bonds and make love to you as to a bride on the wedding night."

"I will not fight you," Nyke responded. He fluttered his eyelashes. He wanted the general to make love to him as a bride. He wanted to make the general love him, to be besotted with him. This was a time that could mean life for him. "You are a handsome man. I could not ask for better."

Lykaios smiled at the compliment, undid Nyke's bounds, and then, to the young blond beauty's surprise, the general gathered him up and carried him over to the copper basin of water and set Nyke down in that and cleansed his body, using the sponge with one hand. With the other he stroked Nyke's cock.

"Sire?" Nyke murmured, a quizzical look on his face, "I think I cannot hold."

"Shush," the general answered in a low, husky voice. "Yes, I want you to spill your seed for me. We will remain here until you do. Do not fight that either."

Nyke laid back in the basin and sighed and moaned and Lykaios slowly stroked him off. With a little cry, Nyke lurched and came, and Lykaios lowered his lips to the young man's and gave him a tender kiss.

"I am glad I did not take you in the maze," he said. "This is better, more fitting for a prince of Phitio."

The general lifted Nyke out of the tub, dried his body with a soft towel, and carried him to the bed. He lay the young man down on his back, crouched full length over him, and kissed down his body, starting with his mouth and ending with the rim of his channel, with long stops at his cock and balls.

Nyke was already writhing and arching his back and rolling his hips with moans and sighs and grasping the general's upper arms and spreading his legs when the general finally was positioning the head of his bull-thick cock at the prince's entrance and pressing in.

Nyke made himself initially tight for the general, but as the phallus marched on, he began to make his channel expand and the muscles therein to start to undulate over Lykaois's member as the Nubian masseur had taught him to do, and the general groaned his fascination at what Nyke's channel was doing to him. Lykaois was lost to the charms of the Phitio prince.

They fucked for hours with intermittent periods of embracing and kissing and murmuring to each other. Nyke was pleasantly satisfied and Lykaios was entranced with his Phitio prince. The virile Lykaios came again and again and again, with Nyke crying for him and clutching his flesh tightly with his fists each time, each time murmuring that he couldn't get enough of the commanding cock and that he never knew it could be this close to paradise lying with a man—and not just a man—with the ruler of the universe, Nyke's universe.

When dawn was finally approaching as was the coast of the state of Brixia, the general was fully Nyke's to command.

He even said so, telling Nyke he would move the young prince into his palace and accord him all of the privileges of his consort.

To this, though, Nyke replied. "No, please, my master. I will lie with you whenever you wish and count it as the greatest privilege, but I ask that my past life be cut off and forgotten. I don't wish to be a prince of Phitio in your country, court, and chambers. Please, you must be my master and I your servant. Take me and train me to whatever you wish. I will become Brixian and my full loyalty will be to you. I will be your slave."

"If you wish it so," the general said with awe, "then it will be so. But only before other men. In private I will be your slave and you my master."

"No, Sire, not even that," Nyke objected. "Your phallus is my master. There is no changing that. All I wish to do is to join your household and to serve you in whatever capacity you find useful."

"You have pleased me, sweet young Nyke, beyond all expectations." At this, Lykaios drew out the gleaming red ruby the size of a sparrows egg and lifted it up for Nyke to gaze up. "As a token of my pleasure at receiving your pledge, I will give you this ruby."

"It's magnificent," Nyke murmured. "But where is it from?"

"It was the price I had to pay to buy you from the governor. And it was to be the prize for whoever found you in the maze. But I find that its worth pales in comparison with your worth to me now, and I wish for you to have it. Consider it a talisman of good fortune from the gods."

And so it was settled before the general's ships reached the harbor of Brixia. And thus Nyke knew it must be. If he was to survive and thrive, there could be no hint of the continued existence of the Phitio prince Nyke reaching the ears of his brother, the crown prince. Nyke needed to totally disappear. For all the crown prince would know, Nyke perished in the assault on the small island he had just left. If the crown prince would not believe that, he would think that Nyke was with his mother on the island of Ia and would expend his effort looking for him there.

True to his talents, Nyke was to find in the months to come that he could serve General Lykaios and Brixia best in the guise of a spy, a role that the court of Phitio had already prepared him well to serve.

Chapter Two: From Brixia to Morini

"I will not buy boys," Xanthos said with a dismissive wave of his hand, although the gleam in his eyes suggested otherwise. "They are unreliable and too inexperienced and they break the crockery while playing their childish games."

"These are no boys, Excellency," the slave master simpered. "These are all past their playing stage and have been trained in service, in special service to a nobleman such as you. Besides, I was told—"

"You did tell me you liked your servants lithe and blond and graceful and small enough not to overturn the furniture, Xanthos," General Lykaios overrode the wheedling of the slave master with a smile. "Come select one of these and be done with it. You have done us a great honor by breaking with Morini and coming to us. We can surely take Morini with your help. Accept our gift of your own serving man; you must be tired of calling upon the senator's servants after he has done with them."

Within, Lykaios was less patient. "Get on with it, you treasonous sea slug," he was thinking and he was not fooled for a second that it was a kitchen servant they were shopping for here.

"Well, I don't know," Xanthos replied as he reached over for his wine cup. As soon as he set it down, Senator Ixsandr's own serving man stepped forward to refill his cup.

Xanthos bounded off his couch. "Well, perhaps if I saw them in the light, and without those loincloths. Come, bring them out on the terrace."

Xanthos pranced out onto the terrace, and the slave master fell in step behind him, tugging on the chains of the three small blond men struggling along behind him and hissing at them to strip down while they were moving to the terrace.

"How can we be sure he'll pick the right one?" Ixsandr whispered to the general, with whom he shared the ruling of Brixia, as he watched Xanthos clucking and prodding the bodies of the young men out on the terrace, spending as long as he thought the Brixia general would tolerate in narrowing his choice to one—in the process getting some pleasure out of all three.

"They are all the right one," Lykaios muttered back, and then he laughed. This was followed by a slight scowl. "But I already regret having included one in the mix. These are among our best-trained spies. Whichever one he picks will keep us apprised of his activities here in Brixia. It was indeed a small victory when he deserted the Morini and came over to us—he was one of their best military minds, despite his stupidity in other matters. But I don't trust a traitor."

"And look at the fool out there," Lykaios continued, changing the subject. "Who does he think he's fooling? He's not picking out a servant. He's picking out someone for his bed. But that's fine. We want him besotted with whoever he selects. He will be more ours with a Brixian catamite than otherwise. Ah, there you are, dear brother Xanthos, back with us again. Boy, refill the flagon of wine for our hero brother. Have you selected? Yes you have, and a very good choice it is too. Nyke, is it not?"

There was a catch in Lykaios throat when he said this. Of course Xanthos would pick Nyke. What man wouldn't? As he feared, Lykaios already regretted including Nyke among the candidates—but Nyke had insisted. He continually wished to show Lykaios his loyalty to the Brixian cause.

Xanthos' selection was standing in the center of the room, demur, his hands at his sides and his face looking shyly at the floor. He was small, as they knew Xanthos really liked, and with blond curls falling down into his face. His body was lithe, that of a graceful dancer, and he was perfectly muscled for the role—not anything either overdone or underdeveloped. He had the cock and balls of a boy, which was particularly in demand this season. His lips were full and sensual and his eyes hazel and sultry, as Lykaios knew without the young man having to raise his head. Of the three, he gave the greatest impression of being innocent and virginal—although Lykaios knew full well this was just a trained pose. He knew this because Lykaios was a master of diplomacy through the art of subterfuge and spying and also because he had very intense and personal experience that belied any claim Nyke might make to being either innocent or, the gods laugh, virginal.

And for the benefit of Brixia, at least, Lykaios was supremely pleased that Xanthos had chosen Nyke, because Nyke was his best sweetmeat spy. If Nyke could not get the armies of Brixia inside the walls of Morini, no one was likely too.

Ixsandr turned to a nearly trembling Xanthos, who was barely able to contain his excitement at the gift of a blond beauty in service to his every need. And Xanthos was aching to have his needs serviced at this point. Ixsandr easily discerned just how aroused Xanthos was. Togas were not built for privacy.

"I regret we cannot indulge ourselves in small talk and wine when your coming to us opens so many possibilities for moving at last against Morini, Xanthos," Ixsandr said in his most magisterial voice. "I must be off to the Senate to arrange the resources General Lykaios and you will, I'm sure, make brilliant use of. And there is much preparation for General Lykaios to complete before you will be needed in counsel. Perhaps you would like to take your new servant back to your apartments and show him how he can best serve you." Senator Ixsandr could hardly keep a straight face at the hidden meanings in his last sentence. He and General Lykaios, the functional dictators of Brixia, wanted Xanthos under their complete power as soon as possible.

"Well, I suppose that might be something I could take a few minutes from more important matters to do," Xanthos said dubiously. But he was already shuffling toward the passageway to his quarters and herding the shy Nyke before him, his hand on the servant's naked buttocks.

"Silly dolt," Lykaios muttered under his breath as he smiled his happy farewells at Xanthos' departure—happy principally at the departure. Then he turned to Ixsandr and said, "I wonder how much flimflamming I need do in war counsel before managing to convince that ass that it's his idea that he is going to return to the court of Morini."

When Ixsandr had all of his plans in order and his minions in tow, he moved down the corridor toward his scheduled meeting of the Senate. As he passed the door into Xanthos' apartments, he saw that Nyke was already at work. Xanthos was lying on his back in the mountain of pillows, and Nyke was astride his pelvis riding his cock like a ship upon the Ionian sea the day after a tempest. From the sounds Xanthos was making, he was quite content with the service his new servant was providing him.

* * * *

"I will not do it; they cannot expect it; what were they thinking?"

Nyke raised his head up from the task at hand and asked, "What, noble sire? What do they expect of you and who is they?" Nyke knew Hades well what this was all about. His assignment was to make Xanthos fall for the plan.

Xanthos was laying on his couch just beyond the line of sunshine flowing in from the terrace of his apartment. Nyke knelt between his thighs at the end of the chaise, Xanthos' legs raised and resting on Nyke's shoulders, and Nyke was working Xanthos' cock in his mouth, sucking on the bulb and flicking the piss slit with his tongue and then taking the whole shaft in with one long slide, listening for the sigh from his master, and then slowly pulling his mouth back. Down again and listening for the sigh. Feeling Xanthos' body go tense and his hips start to jerk, grabbing Nyke's golden curls in his hands and emitting little chirps of pleasure. Nyke taking him down to the root and applying pressure to the root with his teeth while gently squeezing Xanthos' balls in his hand. And then swallowing the spurted semen as quickly as he was able, trying not to gag or to spoil the moment in any other way for his master. Then sitting up and looking down into eyes glazed with the satisfied remembrance.

Eyes that quickly cleared and set into an expression of the spoiled pout.

"Wine, Nyke. Must I tell you whenever my glass nears empty? And it's long past time for my massage. The games this morning were grueling."

"Grueling for your adversaries," Nyke voiced in honeycombed praise as he scrambled off the couch and trotted off for the wine pitcher and the oil, sponge, and marble phallus. That was one thing Xanthos was, though, Nyke had to admit. Prissy and self-possessed as he was, Xanthos was master at the games, and, Nyke assumed, therefore also a champion on the field of battle. Nyke had watched in the stadium and had slowly and involuntarily taken on Xanthos as his champion. His muscled body was beautiful to Nyke as he watched Xanthos win one throw after the other, and when they had returned to the coolness of the senator's villa in the heat of the day, Nyke hadn't minded at all sponging water over Xanthos' body in the bath as Xanthos sat back in the water, lapped Nyke, and raised his hole up and down on a strong, firm cock. That was another thing Xanthos was. Young and virile and quick to recover and ever ready for the fuck.

His strength was also his weakness, though. Xanthos became ever more controllable as Nyke spun a web of lust and want around him.

"You did not tell me what was troubling you," Nyke whispered in Xanthos' ear as he had him laid belly down on the couch and was massaging his neck muscles. Nyke had his own agenda to work to.

"The fools want me to return to Morini and be their spy inside the court—to undermine the Morini from within. Do they have any idea what that would take, what the dangers are?"

"They must, master," Nyke spoke in a soothing voice. "They have devised this as their best stratagem, laying it all, the future of Brixia, on your shoulders. They must trust you very much and must see the great talent that is within you. I think they respect your use to them too much to put you in mortal danger. I have heard that they have great plans for you as a leader."

"Humph," was Xanthos' reply, and then, in a huskier voice, "Yes, that is good, deeper there. Oh yes, and there too."

Nyke had moved his oiled fists down to the small of Xanthos' narrow waist at the back and then down to roll and knead his meaty buttocks. Nyke pulled the cheeks apart as he was working them and bent down and blew on Xanthos' hole, which puckered right up, the action earning a sigh from Xanthos. And then Xanthos was grunting and slowly churning his hips as Nyke's tongue went to the opening.

"Enough," Xanthos growled huskily, and then he turned onto his back, saluting Nyke at three-quarters' staff. "The marble phallus," he murmured.

Nyke oiled up the marble phallus as Xanthos watched with slitted eyes and licked his lips, and then Xanthos, his legs bent, hips rolled up, and a hand encasing Nyke's cock, moaned, as Nyke moved the bulb of the oiled phallus around the rim of Xanthos' opening, slowly worked it inside his channel, and rubbed the smooth tip on Xanthos' prostate. Xanthos was slowly working Nyke's small, thin cock and his pert little balls while Nyke worked both Xanthos' hole with the phallus and his staff with an oiled fist—at first—and then with his mouth, until Xanthos had ejaculated once more and Nyke had swallowed his essence again.

While Nyke was massaging Xanthos' legs and chest after, he endeavored to complete his essential assignment.

"Who but you could bring off such a feat, master? Isn't it, upon reflection, a brilliant plan? And aren't you the perfect man to bring it off? Your story and name will be sung down through the ages."

"I suppose you are right," Xanthos said in a faraway voice, already composing his own song to his personal glory. "But you have had enough rest, you lazy slave. Here, I want you."

As Xanthos sat up and picked the small servant up from the floor with hands encasing his waist and seating him on the couch in front of him and facing him, Nyke worked in the last, burning question he'd been told to have answered. Xanthos was here, but no one in Brixia could tell the senator and general how he had gotten here, how he had gotten out of Morini unnoticed—which may just be the key for getting the army of Brixia inside Morini.

"But it may all be just a dream, you cannot return to Morini. It is too heavily guarded. You cannot get back in. Oh, sire!"

Xanthos had pushed Nyke onto his back below him and barked, "Spread your legs and grab your ankles," and Nyke was groaning at the invasion of his hole by oiled, thick fingers.

"That is no problem for such as I," Xanthos boasted, as he straddled the couch with his legs and grabbed Nyke's hips with his hands. "I will just go back in to Morini the way I came out. And speaking of getting in—"

"Oh, sire, oh, SIRE, OHHHH!" Nyke cried out as Xanthos pulled the youthful torso of the blond servant toward him along the now-slippery couch surface, and his long, thick cock slowly disappeared into a tight ass channel.

Later in the night, when Xanthos was finished cocking Nyke again, they were laid, stretched out on the sleeping divan, bringing their breath back to calm.

"But, what about me, my lord?" Nyke whispered in a small voice. "I don't know how I would live—"

"Hush, hush, my sweet one," Xanthos murmured as He brushed the sex-wet blond curls out of Nyke's face and embraced him closely. "This cock has not had its fill of you either. I will take you to Morini with me."

Nyke cooed and snuggled closer into Xanthos' embrace. This part of the mission accomplished.

* * * *

61

"Master, why are you leading me this way?" Nyke asked in a whisper. "Morini is on the west slope of Mount Fotia. You are leading us to the east."

The night was dark and they had placed sacking on the hooves of the horses and were moving as silently as possible. It was a moonless night, and the only illumination other than the stars was the glow from atop Mount Fotia, which had been smoldering and sending up clouds of ash and noxious fumes since before Nyke was birthed.

"Yes," Xanthos answered with a low laugh. "And why is it that your searchers from Brixia have never found our secret entrance into our city? It's because you look on the wrong side of the mountain."

Hours later, standing on a shelf of rocks outside the yawning entrance to a cavern on the east slope of Mount Fotia, Nyke held back in fear when Xanthos would have plunged right into the mouth of the deep labyrinth.

"This is the Labyrinth of the Underworld, isn't it?" Nyke muttered in awe. "I've never been here, but I have heard of it. Our foretellers came here for signs until they all died of mysterious illnesses. I've heard that to enter here now is to die."

"Yes, it is, and it indeed is a home of the dead," Xanthos answered. "But if you follow me, very close behind me, we will soon be inside Morini. You must trust me, Nyke."

"Yes, yes, I must," Nyke answered. And indeed he had to. His mission was to get inside Morini and return to serve as guide for the Brixian army, or not return at all.

They walked into the dark of the cavern, and Xanthos lit a torch. Nyke saw that ahead was a maze of many choices, many decisions to be made. There were far too many passages leading off from the entrance cavern for him to have any idea which to follow. And it was not in total darkness here, any more than it had been on the trail around the base of the mountain from Brixia. There was a soft glow down some of the passageways and trails of vapors wafting out of the entrances to these shafts as well as others.

Xanthos was doing something strange with the torch. He was not holding it high; he was holding its tip close to the ground and was training his own gaze there as well.

Nyke instinctively moved to his left, assuming the passage they sought was the one farthest away from the ones with the glowing interiors. But as he moved to the entrance, Xanthos grabbed his arm and pulled him back.

"Not that one, little one." He skipped a rock into the dark of the entrance to that passage, and Nyke's stomach turned over as he heard the hollow sound of the rock tumbling down into a hole.

"As I said, stay close to me," Xanthos said.

Far into the Labyrinth, Xanthos lifted an arm and stopped Nyke in his tracks. They were in a cavern from which there were three openings other than the one they had entered.

"It is vital that we be careful at this point," Xanthos said. "There are three choices. All three are winding paths that will take away both your sense of direction and your sense of returning. One entrance, the one of the left, leads nowhere, forever, but deep into the belly of the mountain to who knows where. The center one leads into a path of slow forming noxious gas that will kill a man before he realizes he is being overcome. We take the opening on the right. And as soon as we enter there, watch as you tread along the base of the walls."

Nyke looked down and then he saw them—painted symbols, small and noticeable only if you were watching closely. But they were there, and by following them through the many winding passages and across crystal-columned caverns, at last they came out into the rear room of a small, unoccupied house in the mountainside wall of Morini at the start of a busy and noisy market day.

Nyke was completely surprised as they led their horses through the bustling streets of the city state toward the palaces of the acropolis area. He had been led to believe that the three-year-long siege of Morini by the forces of Brixia had reduced it to a starving cesspool, but, as much as the smell of the place—indeed of any healthy city state in the world—was that of a dung heap, the town looked prosperous and the inhabitants perfectly pleased with themselves. And they seemed pleased with Xanthos too, which was the most shocking to Nyke. He was not seized upon as a deserting traitor but was hailed by the more prosperous-looking citizens, who no doubt knew him, and was given way to with bows and admiring looks by all others, who seemed to know of him.

But then what must be the truth dawned on Nyke. Xanthos was held in such esteem in Morini that the citizens had not been told he had deserted lest this imperil the false sense of security they had all taken upon themselves.

"We shall see what we shall see when we get to wherever Xanthos is leading us, though," Nyke thought.

And when they did, Nyke was not all that surprised that as soon as they strode into the reception hall of the villa, four hefty guards formed up beside Xanthos, with one of them prodding Nyke off to the side as inconsequential. A tall, straight-limbed and imposingly togaed man of many years appeared in the doorway opposite to the entrance to the villa.

"Hail, Consul Aneas," Xanthos boomed out in a voice dripping with affection and totally absent of fear. Nyke admired his courage at this moment.

"So, you return to us, do you, General Xanthos? Enjoy your little excursion, did you? Perhaps you will join me within for a little meeting of the minds."

The consul turned and disappeared from the doorway, and Xanthos followed him, hemmed in closely by four burly, straight-legged, empty-expressioned military guards.

This was what Nyke knew would be one of the trickiest times for him. The plan had never been for Xanthos to regain his place in Morini and serve the interests of Brixia. The functional leaders of Brixia, Senator Ixsandr and General Lykaios, never had any use for Xanthos once he returned. All that they wanted from him was to show Nyke how to get into and out of Morini. And all Nyke wanted to do at this point was to get safely out of the Consul Aneas' villa and back to the Labyrinth of the Underworld while he still had the route of the maze in his mind.

"I wouldn't wait around here, if I were you—not unless you want to share the ordeal that is being meted out to our valorous Xanthos." Nyke turned and found he was looking up into the eyes of a handsome, well-built man with auburn hair and laughing hazel eyes, dressed as a servant, older, taller, and more solid than Nyke was and obviously very comfortable in his environment.

"If you come with me and would like to have food in your mouth and a place to sleep in the lap of luxury, I'll perhaps be able to make a position for you here," the young man said. "My name is Cirillo, and I serve the consul Aneas. But unless you want to be here to explain yourself when the guards reappear, you'd best come with me."

Nyke blindly followed Cirillo into a passageway that led beside a garden atrium and into the bowels of the villa, which was some sort of labyrinth itself from a century of haphazard expansion. They stopped and then walked more gingerly at the sound of lashing and a man crying out. Cirillo paused at the corner of a doorway and motioned Nyke to peek inside.

Xanthos, naked, was on his knees at the foot of a couch, with his lower belly on the edge of a low divan's surface and his torso stretched up to where his arms v'd out above his hanging head and were bound to posts at either side of the couch. The consul Aneas, also naked, and superbly fit for his many years, was crouched over Xanthos' hips and fucking him while half-heartedly lashing at Xanthos' back and buttocks with a many-thonged whip.

After only a glimpse of this, Cirillo took Nyke's hand and led him quickly back into the labyrinth of the villa, where the furnishings became coarser and the rooms smaller and with less access to the sun. When they reached a small room off a side corridor, with a single narrow couch in it, Cirillo pushed Nyke down in a seated position on the couch and turned to him.

"I serve Aneas in every way. Am I to surmise that you have served Xanthos in the same way?"

"Yes," Nyke said. It was no shame and he saw no reason to deny it.

"And are you pleased with Xanthos?"

"What do you mean?"

"I don't mean politically. Hades may have the lot of them for their politics. I serve no man but myself. And if I could leave this hell hole of a city pretending that life is just as it should be as it quietly starves and creeps to its enslavement, I would do so."

"You would go over to Brixia?" Nyke said, trying to fill the tone of his voice with disbelief and censure.

"In a moment's time, yes. They are the ones who live free on the plains as we grovel here inside our trapping walls. But that's not what I meant. I meant does Xanthos have a cock as good as this one?" Cirillo pulled his tunic over his head and stood there in the nude. His body was beautiful, but neither his body nor his cock were any more beautiful than Xanthos' were. Nyke saw no reason to disappoint or alienate this young man who had rescued him from a quite possibly very sticky situation at the entrance to the villa. And, besides, the young man was very nice and Nyke did need a place to hide until he could return to the labyrinth. And, Nyke did like to be fucked; otherwise he would not be in Brixian General Ixsandr's special service.

"No, you are beautiful and manly, and superbly manned," Nyke answered.

Cirillo seemed pleased. "I told you back at the entrance that perhaps I could give you a place here. The perhaps is if you will serve me as well as you have served Xanthos. I know you are no simple wine holder. I know a catamite when I see one. Do you service well?"

"As well as you may wish, sire," Nyke said, as he reached out for the cock Cirillo had been stroking. As Nyke opened his mouth to Cirillo's cock, he was thinking, "My good fortune that you take me for a mere catamite and not for a spy."

When Cirillo lifted Nyke's tunic over his head and pushed his back down onto the couch, Nyke spread and lifted his legs and rolled up his hips, and then gasped and cried out and moaned as Cirillo thrust inside him and made him feel that, indeed, the cock of the consul's man was longer, thicker, and more vigorous than that of Xanthos.

Saying that he could not yet fully trust him, Cirillo kept Nyke bound and imprisoned in his room for several days, appearing occasionally and fucking the beautiful small blond with the curly golden hair until, after purposely letting Nyke go for two days without sex, Nyke begged him for the fuck. Then, deeming Nyke completely within his control, Cirillo released him and let him work in the kitchens during the day and come back to his bed in the evening.

For Nyke's part, he played Cirillo's game, always looking for the opportunity to leave, but being totally lost in the maze of the villa. He would not have been impatient about the time it was taking except that the longer this game went on, the less sure he was that he could renegotiate the Labyrinth of the Underworld.

Cirillo solved that problem for him.

One night while they were languidly fucking, Nyke asked, as innocently as he could, "Were you speaking truthfully that first day when you said you had no allegiance to Morini?"

"Truthfully," Cirillo answered, and then he let loose with a long litany of all of the ills that Morini had done to him and those he had lost.

"Would that I could leave, I would take you with me," Nyke whispered, worried lest the walls have ears. "But I have no idea how to leave."

"I do," Cirillo answered. "There is a way through the Labyrinth of the Underworld. I know it well."

Nyke felt that the gods had been with him in his journey thus far—and, to him, the ruby sewn in the hem of his tunic was the talisman of the gods. His hand went to the lump in his tunic, and Cirillo spied the act.

"What do you have there?"

"As you have opened your secrets to me, I shall open mine to you," Nyke said. With that he unbound the gem and held it up for Cirillo to see.

Cirillo's eyes grew large in awe. "That must be a king's ransom," he muttered.

"Almost, yes," Nyke said with a little laugh. "Isn't it beautiful?"

"Where did you get it?"

"Fate brought it to me, and I have come to believe that it will guide me through the labyrinth."

"The labyrinth? I told you that I would guide you through the labyrinth."

"And you too have become as a ruby to me, Cirillo," Nyke whispered and gave his lover a kiss on the mouth. "But I had meant the labyrinth of life."

"I am not sure there is a path through life's labyrinth," Cirillo said as Nyke returned the ruby to its hiding place.

"Nor I," Nyke whispered with a sad sigh. "I have come to believe that I cannot count on there being more than a here and now. And that being my belief, could you make love to me again—here and now."

For now, both of the young men forgot all about labyrinths and rubies.

* * * *

Weeks later Cirillo was standing on the terrace of Senator Ixsandr's villa in Brixia, waving to the vanguard of the army of Brixia as it was departing the city for the eastern side of Mount Fotia. At the head of the army was General Lykaios, and beside him rode the servant Nyke, put in the front of the column as guide through the Labyrinth of the Underworld.

Well into the Labyrinth, in the cavern giving three choices of turning. General Lykaios turned to Nyke with a question in his eyes.

"Bear straight ahead, my general," Nyke said. "That is the true route." Nyke had not been fooled by the remarking of passages by the Morini forces. When last he'd passed by, he had marked the entrances himself with piles of stones near the entrances that only he could interpret. He knew exactly which opening he wanted the army of Brixia to take.

The Brixian forces of General Lykaios filed quietly into the passage that Xanthos had told Nyke was the twisting choice of slow choking death from noxious gases but that now was marked as the safe passage. Nyke waited for some hours, fearful that the rear formations of the attack force would have turned around at some sign the advance guard gave of a choking death—or because Xanthos had lied to him. When none returned, though, Nyke crept back to the entrance of the labyrinth to wait and watch, and start his journey back to Phitio. As he waited, he fingered the lump caused by the ruby sewn into the hem of his tunic. It would be an arduous journey through Cenopolis and back to the Phitio island Ia to join his mother and his other supporters. For all he knew his father, the king, was dead now and the time was ripe to rise against his brother. In Nyke's heart he knew that the ruby would help him win through.

Cirillo also waited until dark back in the city of Brixia, giving Brixia's army time to enter the maw of the labyrinth. Then he stole along the corridor of the senator's villa, meeting no one to challenge him, as Senator Ixsandr had assured him would be the case. Cirillo had spent considerable effort cultivating the senator since he and Nyke had escaped from Morini and arrived in Brixia. Cirillo had become Senator Ixsandr's favorite, which was why Cirillo had not accompanied the forces of General Lykaios as auxiliary guide—there had been quite a row over that between the senator and the general, but the senator simply would not part with his new lover.

As Cirillo massaged Ixsandr's back, his mind wandered to the image of the forces of Brixia now entering the maw of the labyrinth and following the signs at the base of the wall, the signs that Morini's consul, Aneas, had caused to be reset after he and Nyke had passed through, the reset signs that would pull the Brixians ever deeper, ever more confusingly into the heart of the volcano and the welcoming arms of its noxious fumes.

Ixsandr raised his hips, which was a sign for Cirillo to pull his cock through and stroke it as his lips went to Ixsandr's hole, opening it up for the last cocking. Once Ixsandr was moaning and begging for the thrust, Cirillo reached under the couch and then crawled over Ixsandr and mounted his hips and thrust inside him. Ixsandr yelped and cried out and clawed at the sides of the couch as Cirillo's cock thrust inside his channel and, with each of those thrusts, Cirillo's dagger thrust into Ixsandr's back.

Across the plain, on the western slope of the glowing Mount Fotia, the Morini consul, Aneas, had just finished fucking and whipping his lover, Xanthos, the two now exhausted after a coupling that brought out the depths of passion in both of them. Aneas unbound Xanthos, and they stretched out on the sleeping couch in each other's arms, as Aneas kissed the welts on his lover's torso.

"There has been no alarm from the street," Xanthos murmured. "That is a good sign. None of General Lykaios' Brixian soldiers have made it through the labyrinth and to the wall. We have men in force there just in case, but there seems nothing for them to do. Cirillo has done well. He sent word that he would take care of Senator Ixsandr personally. Brixia decapitated in one blow. We can open the gates of the city again."

"Yes, but it is a big price for Cirillo to pay," the Consul Aneas murmured. "I did so enjoy Cirillo. And he was the best of my special spies."

"No, master," Xanthos answered. "Cirillo should be safe if he's kept his wits about him and the gods are favorable. I told him to steal out of Brixia in the confusion and to remain in the wilderness at a town called Theron for a week. By then we will have remarked the passage through the labyrinth. We have it marked by cuttings as well as the painted symbols, so we can easily restore the route. Cirillo will be back in your arms soon and with many an interesting secret to tell us about Brixia."

As the two Morini's cooed and kissed and ran their hands over each other's bodies in anticipation of the return of Aneas' man strength and desire to be moving deep inside Xanthos, a figure felt safe at last to move from the shadows near at hand into the deeper shadows of the chamber and beyond. As he silently glided out of the chamber, the consul's night steward, Dymas, kept going over the phrase in his mind so that he would not forget it, "Cirillo in the village of Theron." He would go directly to his messenger who would then contact the men of Cenopolis who lingered outside of the city, to the north of Mount Fotia. The time was ripe for his city, Cenopolis. Not only was Brixia crippled by the loss of its army and of its functional rulers, but Morini also was ripe for the picking in its false sense of security. And the spy Cirillo was the key. As ultimately a spy for Cenopolis instead of Morini, there was so much Cirillo could tell the men of that state. Not only the secrets of Brixia but the way into Morini as well.

Chapter Three: From Morini to Cenopolis

Although Nyke had some sense of the direction he must take to reach the shore of Ia, opposite the archipelago state of Phitio, getting there, through the rough terrain and hostile environment of land under the control of the state of Cenopolis would, he knew, be extremely difficult. Nyke wondered if Cenopolis was still attacking the islands of Phitio. If so, their forces in their own country would be weaker. But then he'd heard that no country in the region had the military force that Cenopolis did.

Pointing his face to the sea, Nyke started out across the uninhabitable scrub land, finding food and water as he was able to do along the way.

Thus it was that he was in a weakened condition when he came upon a small caravan of traders headed toward the east. When he hailed them, they stopped, and three big, strapping men came down off their sturdy, big-muscled horses and gathered around Nyke. To him they were barbarians, perhaps from the north. Big, hairy beasts with flaming red hair that descended to their shoulders and long, bushy beards. They wore coarse-cloth tunics over fur trousers and big, black leather boots.

Nyke did not like the way they were circling around him and he was about to bid them farewell and move away when he heard mumbling and whining from one of two rough carts being pulled by oxen behind the traders' horses. The cart from which he heard the noises was more a cage on wheels, with black drapes hanging inside the walls, shielding whatever was therein from view.

Nyke looked over to this vehicle and thought he could see the rough-weave draping cloth stirring and a dark face looking out.

"So, you would like to accompany us into the capital city of Cenopolis, would you?" the one who appeared to be the barbarians' leader asked. He was wearing a big grin and he had reached for and was fingering the hem of Nyke's tunic, much too close, Nyke feared for the lump that was hiding the ruby he carried. "Fine cloth for someone journeying in the wild," he said.

"No, I am not a traveler," Nyke said. "I was just walking ahead of my compatriots. We are headed for our military encampment nearby." Nyke had decided that these were not men he wanted to travel with, even if they had food and water to share with him and horses and wagons to ride on occasionally in his journey.

"I am not so sure there is a military encampment near here—and you look too sweet and tender to be a soldier," the leader of the traders said. "You look more like a sweetmeat to be enjoyed."

Nyke took a step away from the northern barbarian, who had come quite close to him. The musky scent of the man was both repelling and intoxicating.

The sound of a shriek split the tension of the air, and, startled, Nyke turned to look at the cage-like cart. The black drape was drawn aside and a small Nubian man was shrieking. "Run. They are evil."

Nyke didn't have a chance to run, however. At a signal from the chief trader, the other two were at Nyke's side and holding fast on his arms, and the leader of the traders was raising his tunic over his head to reveal massive chest and arm muscles and a torso covered with curly red hair. He strode to the back of the cart and pulled bolts open and hopped nimbly into the cart interior. The cart thrashed back and forth briefly, accompanied by the screams of the Nubian prisoner.

Then the trader was hopping down from the cart again and turning and grabbing the ankles of two black legs and pulling them beyond the tailgate of the cart. The Nubian appeared to be trying to sit up on the back edge of the cart when the trader had let go of his legs to untie and lower the flap of his own leather codpiece and let a formidable thick cock tumble out, but as the Nubian sat up and made to jump from the back of the cart, the trader drew back his arm and punched the Nubian in the face, snapping his body back into the covered cart. After that all Nyke could see were the hips and legs of the small black man, as the trader fisted the Nubian's ankles and spread his legs and started pistoning his channel with a hard cock. No sounds were coming from the Nubian now, so Nyke concluded that he had been knocked unconscious by the blow to his face.

When the trader was done and had unceremoniously pushed the black legs back into the cart, he turned and looked at Nyke with a grin on his face.

"Will we make sport of this one too, Gregor?" one of the barbarians holding Nyke asked.

"Not now. We have been stopped long enough. We must press on to an encampment for the night. There we will make sport."

One of the men holding Nyke mumbled, "Sure, you get your pleasure, but we—"

"What was that that you said?" the trader leader growled.

"Nothing, Gregor, nothing," the other man immediately answered. Nyke could feel the man shudder and this was all he needed to know about who was in control in this band—and how cruel he could be.

"Haul the golden-haired sweetpie up here," Gregor ordered, and Nyke was picked up between the other two, manhandled over to the back of the cart, and thrown in. He landed nearly on top of the body of the unconscious Nubian and scuttled to the far end of the cart as the door was shut and the bolt shot home.

The light was dim inside the cart, but there were tears in the black drapes and Nyke could see—and smell—well enough to determine he wanted to avoid the other back corner of the cart. He was jolted and fell onto his side as the cart lurched into motion, but he was able to grasp the side panels enough soon to keep his body steady as the caravan resumed its track across the scrubby terrain.

After a while the Nubian began to moan softly and then he was awake and sitting in one of the front corners of the cart and staring dully at Nyke.

"I thank you for trying to warn me," Nyke said at length, knowing that the assault the small, black man had suffered was from an attempt to help him.

"You will be sorry you hailed this caravan," the Nubian answered in a voice with a thick accent whose land Nyke couldn't identify.

"How do you come to be here?" Nyke asked.

"I was stolen from my family in the south some time ago and taken north. And now I am being taken east to be sold as a slave. If I live that long."

Nyke said nothing to that, and after a brief pause the Nubian continued. "There were three of us when we started for the east. The other two were used up and sold. I can only believe I too will be used up soon."

"Used up?" Nyke asked. But there was no answer to that, and soon the two sank into their own thoughts and did not speak again.

Some time after the caravan had stopped, the bolt to the door scraped open and the door was thrust aside and one of the traders muttered, "You, sweetmeat. Come outside." Nyke did not move, though, and the man growled. "You do not want me to come in there and get you."

Nyke moved forward then as the trader shoved a metal plate of food across the floor of the cart and the Nubian leaned forward and snapped it up and began to eat greedily from it. When Nyke reached the back of the cart, strong hands grabbed him by the arms and roughly pulled him from the cart. "You eat later. After the sport," the trader muttered.

The sun was already down and the traders had set up their camp, had a fire going, and apparently had already eaten. All three were stripped down to their fur trousers with the leather codpieces and their black boots. Their torsos were bulging, with veins standing out as there was no fat for them to go through, and glistened with sweat from the work they'd done to settle the camp for the evening. The horses were grazing beyond the rim of the stand of trees the camp had been set up in. The beasts' saddles were spaced just inside the circle of light that came from the open fire.

Without ceremony, Nyke was stripped of his tunic and loincloth and pushed over to near the fire and forced belly down, bent over the seat of one of the massive saddles. He knew what was coming and he was determined not to beg or give them the satisfaction of hearing him scream. He would do all of his screaming inside.

The three of them worked on binding his wrists and ankles and stretching his extremities out and staking them to the ground so that he was spread-eagled over the saddle with his bare buttocks elevated. With the three of them there, he had no hope of resisting. So, he didn't.

For the next hour, the three of them took turns fucking him from the rear, and although he could not help but groan and grunt and moan, he did not give them the satisfaction of crying out or screaming.

After the three had had their sport, they released him and let him lean against the saddle and eat and drink a mean meal.

"Gregor, look at this. There is something inside his tunic," one of the traders who had been playing with Nyke's tunic said. All three traders gathered around and stared in awe at the ruby they had found.

"I knew you would bring us good fortune," Gregor declared with a laughing voice. "And such a sweet ass you have. We may get nearly the worth of this from you in the markets of Baghdad."

"Only if you do not use me up before reaching Baghdad," Nyke answered dryly. For that, he got a backhand slap across his face. But he also received a speculative look from Gregor, and although he was taken by each of the three in the evening again and then lay under Gregor, his buttocks pinned to the ground under one of the carts by a slow-pumping cock, at night for the next several days, Nyke felt that he was not abused as he might have been, an observation also made to him by the Nubian, who began to voice hope that he too might survive to reach Baghdad.

Two days later, the caravan stopped while it was still light and Nyke was let out of the cart—although the Nubian wasn't—earlier than usual and was staked out with a collar and chain beside a small waterhole, as the traders set about establishing an encampment. When one of the traders came close enough for Nyke to speak to him without Gregor hearing them, he asked, "Why have we encamped early? Where are we?"

"We are at the eastern border of the land of Cenopolis now. Gregor favors this encampment as he believes the temple ahead is bewitched and provides good fortune protection to him for the journey into the wilderness, where the going will be rougher and the bandits more plentiful. From here we turn south to the city of Cenopolis before entering the wilderness."

"The temple?" Nyke asked.

"Do you not see the Temple of the Son over there? That marks the far reaches of the Cenopolis state."

Nyke looked the short distance across a plain and saw a stepped temple made out of smooth, black stone that rose to the height of at least twenty men. He could not see an entrance to the temple and thus assumed they were looking at the back side of the edifice. "A temple to the sun? I didn't realize the Cenopoli were sun worshipers."

"No, it is the temple to the son of the king. They don't worship the sun, but they nonetheless have strange customs here. But you need not worry about that. You should be asking me about the size of men's cocks in Baghdad." At that, the trader laughed at his own joke and moved off. Thirsty, Nyke moved over to the side of the waterhole and leaned down and drank greedily.

When the traders came for him, Nyke was prostate on the ground, moaning and burning up with fever, his skin red and puffy and covered with blotches.

All he heard was a cry of "It's the plague. It must be the plague" before he passed into unconsciousness.

* * * *

Nyke was in a haze when he regained some semblance of consciousness and for some time later he was not quite sure what was reality and what merely his fever playing sport with him. He opened his eyes to a vision of a god. The man was tall and willowy, although his musculature was strong and hard. He was white against the blue of the sky. That's how Nyke would have described him if he had been asked—white. His skin was fair and his hair was stark white. He was of an indeterminate age, but surely not young. He probably was old, but he moved with a smooth grace and was hard of body, which belied the vision of a wrinkled old man. His torso was bare. He wore a necklace around his neck made of white crystals. His hips and legs were swathed in a long, pristine-white skirt and the sandals on his feet were ribboned with white.

He was leaning over Nyke's prone body with a basin at his side and he was sponging Nyke off with a cool liquid that chilled at the touch. Where it did not touch, however, Nyke's body was burning hot.

The man was humming a low-toned, haunting tune as he sponged Nyke's body. All of this was quite clear in Nyke's mind later when he recovered from his fever and found that he was then lying, clothed in a white tunic, in the same place he had been lying when he became ill, but now he was lying on a clean mat with a jug of water and a sack of food beside him and a placard on a stake at the edge of the waterhole with a large X painted on it—a sign he took as a warning to not drink from the waterhole, which gave him an explanation of why he had been sick.

What was not so clear, however, was the image of the man releasing the chained collar at Nyke's throat with a mere touch of his hand and later, the sensual sensation that the man was working his cock with his mouth and taking Nyke to a pleasurable climax.

There certainly was no man there when Nyke awoke, but someone most certainly had been there and had left Nyke in far more comfort than the traders had left him in, at the edge of the waterhole. Nyke felt weak but the fever had passed as had the red blotches on his skin.

The traders had also departed. For this, Nyke was grateful, although he was in despair that he had lost the ruby and he worried about the plight of the little Nubian. Upon thought, though, he reasoned that perhaps his parting from the band had all been from the good fortune of possessing the ruby as long as he had it. This left worrying questions about whether this protection—and thus his good fortune—had deserted him now.

He sat on the mat for a good part of the day, but no white-haired spirit appeared. Near dusk, he decided he needed to move from the waterhole and, taking up the jug of water and the sack with what remained of the food he had been provided, he walked to the shadow of the Temple of the Son.

Nyke circled the base of the temple three times, not finding an opening, until he noticed a place where an inscription had been carved into the wall of the temple. As he approached, he noticed that at this point, the stone rim at ground level that surrounded the base of the temple had indentations of two feet in it. Putting his feet in the indentations, Nyke leaned over and read the inscription.

Proceed on the right footing
But turn to contrariness
And behold the rays of the son.

The young prince of Phitio contemplated the riddle for some moments and then moved his right foot forward to where it nudged at an irregular-shaped block of stone at the base of the temple. He heard a rumbling noise from within and the stone in front of his face parted to each side, providing an opening of a high door. Without hesitation, Nyke entered the temple, only to be confronted with openings to three passages. He had led with the right foot and had been told to be contrary, so he took the passage to the left and started to ascend a stone staircase. At each necessity to decide between two turnings, he took the contrary turning—the opposite one to the one he had taken before—and thus a series of staircases led him to a stone-walled chamber near the apex of the temple.

Entering the chamber, Nyke spied the white-haired apparition that had given him succor by the waterhole. The man was sitting on a stone throne raised above and beyond a solid cubical stone altar. Although the man looked regal where he sat, he also looked uncomfortable sitting there.

"It is not my throne, you know," he said in a slightly weary voice. "It is much too large for me, and I have failed. But this is where I will be sitting when they come for what they will not find."

"You are the one who saved me . . . at the waterhole . . . are you not?"

"You were in no real danger. At least not from the water you drank from the spoiled spring. You were in greater danger from the men I saw near you before you took sick. The water of the spring inconveniences; it does not kill. And even in its inconvenience it frightens more than damages. But I am glad that it did its job of freeing you from those men."

"How did you know I was there?"

"I saw you from that balcony over there. And at first I thought you were he, returning, saving Cenopolis and me as well. You look so much like . . . Well, it was a failing on my part for leaving my post and coming to you. And it is strictly forbidden that a foreigner enter this chamber. But as I am piling failing upon failings, I'm content that I did and that you are here. I could not tell until I came close that you were not he. But of course you could not have been."

This man was as much a riddle, Nyke thought, as the secret of the entrance to the temple was.

"Are you the priest of this temple?"

"Alas, I am. All of the miseries to come fall on my shoulder."

"What is the purpose of this temple, might I ask? Why is it known as the Temple to the Son?"

"This is where the king aspirant—the son of the king of Cenopolis—resides until he is called to his kingship. Here he is safe from the world and from the intrigues of men."

The priest suddenly stopped and looked sharply at Nyke. "You are no mere slave, are you? You are royalty in your own right."

Nyke squirmed. "I have been told that somewhere in my past—"

"You could not have entered the temple otherwise. It is not just the riddle; the door would not open for anyone but a male of royal blood. I knew from the moment I saw you lying out there by the spring that I must go to you."

Nyke spoke up, wishing to deflect where this questioning was headed. If the priest were an official of Cenopolis, he would not welcome the knowledge that a prince of the state of Phitio stood before him and had reached the inner sanctum of the heir to the throne of Cenopolis.

"If this is the safe haven of the crown prince of Cenopolis, where is the man? Are you he?"

"No, I am not the crown prince. He is there, before you."

Nyke looked, but he saw no prince—only an altar.

"He is there, in the sarcophagus standing between us. He is dead this three years. And that is my failure. When they come for him, they will only find me. And I will be torn limb from limb for not keeping the crown prince alive and well. And now I must—"

The priest had stood up from the throne that was not his and taken a step, but then he began to fall.

Nyke ran to his side and held him up. The man motioned to a door at the side of the chamber, and Nyke helped him through there, to find a bed chamber. He laid the man on the bed.

"That flagon, there, my son," the priest whispered. "An elixir. It rejuvenates me."

Nyke reached for the flagon and put it to the priest's lips, and it did, indeed, immediately start invigorating the man. It was like years flowed away and his muscles were hardening and his grip on Nyke's arms became stronger. He was looking into Nyke's eyes, and Nyke recognized that look. A carnal look of longing and wanting.

"You must leave now," the man hissed through his teeth. "It has been so many years. And you are such a beauty. I cannot. The elixir. It has side properties. You must flee from me."

This man had saved Nyke's life, and Nyke had nothing to offer in return now—nothing but the comfort of his body. He reached a hand through the folds of the priest's skirting and felt the rock hardness of the man's want and need. The elixir had made him a giant of a man.

Gently, Nyke unknotted the skirt at the priest's waist and spread the cloth away from the man's body. The priest was begging Nyke to leave with his mouth but entreating him to stay with his eyes, while his fists clutched at Nyke's waist and buttocks under his tunic.

Nyke pulled his tunic over his head and rose up over the priest's body, straddling his hips, and spent a long, gloriously painful time lowering his channel on the magically enhanced phallus and rode the priest's cock into the late darkness of the night, each enjoying countless ejaculations, thanks to the magic of the elixir.

* * * *

The two Cenopolis spies, Cirillo, escaping from Brixia after killing its co-ruler, Senator Ixsandr, while General Lykaios marched Brixia's soldiers to their deaths in the Labyrinth of the underworld, and Dymas, having stolen out of the chambers of Consul Aneas of Morini, met in the designated village of Theron. Brixia was now crippled and, together, they rode hard for the capital city of Cenopolis. They arrived there amid chaos. The old king was dying.

However, the two spies' impassioned pleas of how advantageous it would be to attack both Brixia, and, ultimately Morini as well, in their time of weakness, prevailed in the ruling councils of Cenopolis. The country would need to almost strip its own defenses bare as the siege of the main islands of Phitio continued and some of the smaller islands of that archipelagic state were occupied by Cenopolis forces, however. And since the recommendations came from Cirillo and Dymas, it was these two councilor spies who were charged with taking the risks involved. Dymas was charged with raising an army and marching on Brixia posthaste. For Cirillo, however, the task was assigned to take a small force north to the Temple of the Son and to bring the crown prince back to the city. Even if he hurried, many were afraid, he would not make it home before the death of the king.

While Dymas gathered his troops and got on the road for Brixia, Cirillo started out for the north. Not far north of the capital city, he and his men ran across a band of three traders from the lands of the north. Cirillo had been warned to watch out for bandits and for a particular band of Morini spies.

The traders at first tried to veer off the post trail, which was their undoing. His suspicions raised, Cirillo led his men to overtake the small caravan.

"We are mere traders traveling through on our way to trade goods and slaves in the markets of Baghdad," declared Gregor in a wheedling voice, with his eyes downcast.

81

"By what road did you enter Cenopolis?" Cirillo asked.

Gregor made the mistake of lying. He had approached Cenopolis from the northwest, but he assumed that the Cenopolis feared and hated the barbarian lands in that direction, so he answered, "Through Morini, my lord."

This blunder led Cirillo to order a search of the caravan. An initial search revealed there were only the three traders, but while Cirillo's men roughly pulled apart the baggage and then turned to searching the bodies of the traders themselves, Cirillo did a circle turn of the traders' horses and carts and returned to face Gregor and ask, "You said you were trading slaves. I see none in your carts."

"No, my lord," Gregor answered with downcast eyes, as he began to panic at the efficient search by Cirillo's soldiers of his own person, "We had three Nubians, but, we sold them for a good price along the way."

Cirillo was about to follow that up, when one of his men who was searching Gregor blurted an oath and lifted an object up for Cirillo to see what he had taken from the inner folds of Gregor's tunic. "My lord, look at this. Have you ever seen a ruby this big and perfect."

Cirillo's eyes narrowed. "Yes, as a matter of fact, I have." He looked sternly at Gregor now and said, "Where did you acquire this?" And not waiting for an answer he went on to demand, "Where is the young golden-haired man you took this ruby from?"

Gregor began to cower and went down on his knees. "It was a traveler who attached himself to our caravan for a few days, my lord. He died on the road. We only took the gem as he had no further use for anything in this world."

"Where? Where did this man die? And what did he die from? Be very careful how you answer, trader, because your very life hangs on my belief in what you say."

"It was at a poisoned spring near the Temple of the Son, in the north of your kingdom. We did not know the spring was poisoned and he was the first to drink. He fell down dead beside the spring. There was nothing we could do for him. Upon my ancestors, I am telling you the truth. We did not murder this man."

Cirillo tried hard to hide his confusion and dismay. He had liked Nyke and had enjoyed cocking him immensely—but he had thought that he had sent him to his death along with the forces of the Brixian general Lykaios in the labyrinth of the underworld. He had a spark of happiness at the thought that Nyke had escaped death at least at that time, but then he became worried that this might mean that Lykaios and his army had survived too and that Dymas and his forces were attacking a country that still had the bulk of its army along with its chief strategist.

"What did you do with the young man's body?" Cirillo asked, his voice full of malice and threat.

"We didn't do anything with the body, my lord. I am sorry, but he appeared as having a plague. We dared not touch him. He should still be lying by the waterhole."

Cirillo was going near to there anyway, so, splitting his company and sending the traders back to the city of Cenopolis with half his men, to be imprisoned until Gregor's story could be verified, he and the rest of the company rode hard for the Temple of the Son.

At the waterhole, Cirillo found no body of Nyke. Approaching the temple and not being of royal blood, Cirillo had to hail the priest of the temple with trumpets to get his attention and gain entry.

The white-haired priest, looking well-satisfied and happy, met Cirillo at the entrance door.

"What brings you to the Temple of the Son?" the priest asked in his official voice. Such a contingent from the capital could only mean one thing—that the king was dead or near death and the crown prince, who the priest had been charged with raising and preparing for his kingship, was now needed to take up his rule. For some strange reason, this did not visibly concern the priest, who just a few days before had been lamenting his undoing because he had no crown prince to produce.

"Come this way," the priest said. "I will lead you to Crown Prince Lucius."

The priest turned and led Cirillo and his men up through the maze of turnings and stairs until they came to the central chamber at the top and the priest declared, "Behold your Prince Lucius," and bowed and let Cirillo pass.

Both Cirillo and the prince sitting on the throne had astonished expressions on their faces, but neither uttered words that would be anyone's undoing.

"Withdraw, all of you," Cirillo demanded of the priest and his own soldiers, and the priest led the soldiers through a side door, saying he would find something to refresh them with.

"So, you are a prince now, are you?" Cirillo asked as he approached the throne.

Nyke, who indeed had always been a prince, answered, "The priest and I thought it best. He said that I closely resembled Prince Lucius and, unfortunately, Prince Lucius died of natural causes some years ago. So, what you need to think upon Cirillo—and I suppose this means you were a spy of Cenopolis all along or are a spy against Cenopolis now—is whether Cenopolis wants the stability of a prince who actually lives or one who is dead and entombed in this sarcophagus sitting on the floor between us."

Cirillo stood in contemplation for a few moments and then answered in a strong, steady voice, "I see that you and the priest have a strong case, and, thinking of the needs of Cenopolis, I think I can see my way to falling in with this arrangement."

"I think that is best and that you are being wise, Cirillo."

"Of course," Cirillo continued, with a sly smile on his face, "If you are to rule in another man's place, I could only let you do so if I stood behind you and guided you."

Now it was Nyke's turn to pause for contemplation. At length, though, he answered, "I can see the wisdom of that. And I had no objection to your ruling my body. We can continue in that vein. I am content with that. I must ask you, however, how you found me."

"I would have found you here anyway," Cirillo answered. "I came to fetch a prince, and it is a prince I will fetch. But I also believed I would find you here because of how I happened upon this." At that point he took the sparrow-egg-sized ruby out of the folds of his tunic and lifted it up for Nyke to see.

"Ah, my good luck charm," Nyke said, holding his hand out. Cirillo hesitated, but then he bowed and returned the ruby to Nyke's hand. "I was premature in thinking that this had stopped bringing me luck," Nyke then said. "You have apprehended the traders from the north then?"

"Yes, and may I assume they did you harm while you journeyed with them."

"Yes, they did. And was there a Nubian slave with them when you arrested them?"

"No, there was not."

"A pity," Nyke said. "Life can be cruel. May I assume they will never leave whatever prison you are sending them to."

"Yes, Prince Lucius. As you wish, your highness." Cirillo bowed low. There was a twinkle in his eye. "We might as well start now, don't you think?"

"Yes, but perhaps we can take the procession back to the capital city slowly. There is so much I should know about the kingdom I shall be ruling."

Chapter Four: From Cenopolis to the Labyrinth's Center

On the road back to the Cenopolis capital city, Prince Lucius assured Cirillo that the forces of the Brixian general Lykaios had perished in the labyrinth under the mountain while trying to sneak into Morini—and thus that the army sent under Dymas to attack Brixia need not be warned to expect a greater defense than would be anticipated.

"Be that as it may," Cirillo answered, "I fear that Dymas, having served consul Aneas of Morini, may be all too familiar with the Brixia captive Nyke. With your permission, once you have been crowned and life in the capital has settled down, I believe I should be sent to . . . consult . . . with Dymas."

"I agree that this would be wise," Nyke said. To himself, though, he began to weave plans of his own.

No one in Cenopolis other than the priest left behind at the Temple of the Son having seen Prince Lucius since infancy, Nyke had no trouble, with Cirillo's help, in being accepted as the new king of Cenopolis.

Upon General Dymas' victory in Brixia, Cirillo and another general sent to relieve Dymas of his command so that he could return to Cenopolis for a victory procession, departed for Brixia. The new general was then to use the labyrinth under the mountain again—this time following Nyke's own markings—to press an attack against the state of Morini.

Before the contingent left, however, the new king called upon the services of the handsome and virile lieutenant of Cirillo's guard force in his bed chamber, timing his visits to avoid those of Cirillo's.

The lieutenant was a tall, handsome brute, younger even than the king. And he was always looking so serious and standing so stiff at attention in the presence of the king. "Lucius" could not be sure that he was sexed at all, although from the moment the new king saw Braxius, he wanted him—and he wanted to see him when his staff was as stiff as his bearing.

Lucius set the discovery of what Braxius might do for him on one warm, lazy afternoon when Cirillo had traveled to inspect the troops on the eastern border. He would be gone for at least three nights.

The king requested some special entertainment in his chambers and, no, he declared, he didn't need a large contingent of bodyguards around. Braxius would do.

Lucius lay naked and pleasuring himself on his bed as a young male dancer danced sensuously for him in the center of the chamber. Braxius was standing stiff and serious beside the bed. But, happily, Lucius could see as the dancer became ever more intimate with himself in the dance that some parts of Braxius were becoming stiffer than other parts.

When Lucius motioned the dancer to the bed and drew the dancer's cock inside him and encircled the dancer's waist with his legs and the two moaned a writhing dance upon the bed, Lucius was pleased to see that Braxius, although still standing at attention, was trembling and breathing heavily.

Afterward, Lucius declared that he wanted a wrestling match out in the courtyard and that Braxius being the only worthy opponent nearby, the king wished to wrestle with his lieutenant of the guard.

They grappled, both naked. Braxius was tentative and was set on falsely showing the king off as more accomplished than he, until Lucius taunted him with his tongue, slapped him with an open palm, and grabbed his balls and squeezed. Braxius was pushed over the edge of restraint and became like a mad man and fought like a tiger, pinning a laughing Lucius to the ground and forcing his pelvis between the king's readily yielding thighs and splitting the king's buttocks with the strong, hard sword jutting out from his belly, thrusting again and again, not realizing what he was doing, although Lucius certainly realized and appreciated what he was doing. Braxius grunted and gave a look of astonishment as he came. But as he tried to pull away from the terrifying thing he had done, Lucius laughed a low throaty laugh, wrapped his legs around Braxius' waist, and clenched the lieutenant's sheathed cock with the muscles of his channel, beginning an undulating motion of those muscles on the virile young cock as, panting heavily, Braxius quickly recovered his hardness and began thrusting anew.

Afterward, they lay there, panting, Lucius mewing and Braxius slowly, alarmingly coming back to his senses.

"My lord," Braxius muttered in shock.

"Again, my savior of the mighty sword," Lucius murmured. "I command you. Again. And take no prisoners, no quarter. The king commands."

And Braxius did as commanded, then and later that night, and the night following that, so that by the time Cirillo returned from the frontier, Braxius was fully vested as the king's lover on the king's command.

When Cirillo and his contingent departed for Brixia, the understandings between the king and Cirillo of what mission lay ahead differed in some slight, but significant way from the understanding between the king and his lieutenant, Braxius, of the mission. Alas, treachery was uncovered in Brixia. Cirillo, understanding that Braxius was to cover his escape from the side of a dying Dymas, was, instead, caught by Braxius and his men escaping from the assassination of Dymas and was, himself, dispatched by the lieutenant of his guard.

When the lieutenant returned to Lucius, he was assigned to exclusive duties to the person of his king until such time, being completely besotted by the charms of King Lucius, he was suborned to the new king's schemes and sent on a secret mission to the island of Ia, in the Phitio archipelago. There, having presented a ruby the size of a sparrow's egg as a symbol of identification to the Second Queen of Phitio on the island of Ia, and after the emissary who had been sent with him, the priest of the Temple of the Son, had closeted alone with the Second Queen for consultations, Braxius negotiated an agreement with the queen and her allies that they would happily help bring an end to the Cenopolis siege of the main island capital of Phitio from the inside and capitulate to the rule of King Lucius of Cenopolis. All that they asked was that the king spend part of his year in the capital of Phitio and that he be known there as King Nyke.

The emissary, Braxius, thought these were strange points of agreement indeed, but, as they favored his own king, he was happy to conclude the treaty.

And thus it was that the new ruler of Phitio was undermined from within, and went to his death a little more than a year after his father died, and that King Lucius of Cenopolis, known as King Nyke in Phitio, soon became the consolidated ruler over not only Cenopolis and Phitio but Brixia and, ultimately, Morini as well.

When asked in later years how it felt to be the ruler over so many kingdoms, the king would take a ruby the size of a sparrow's egg out of the folds of his robes, lift it to catch the light, turn and smile and wink at his mother queen, and murmur, "It feels like at long last and against all odds attaining the center of the labyrinth."

* * * *

General Braxius was sitting at his table, looking at his visage in the mirror and preparing for the king's call to attend him in the royal bedchamber when he heard the scratching at the secret door behind the tapestry.

"Enter," he bellowed, half expecting that he knew who was coming to him in secret at this time of night. He turned and looked at the servant who materialized from the shadows and was not surprised. "I thought that was you I saw serving at the banquet. I wondered who they would send, but it is good that it is someone I would recommend."

Braxius had trained with this man in his home country of Treadia, the country beyond the northern boundaries of Morini. They had both been well prepared to serve their king in secret in the courts of other lands. Braxius had been more fortunate than most. He not only had gone undetected, but he had also wormed his way into the bed of the king of Cenopolis, having conveniently dispatched his competition in a way that only enhanced his standing with the young king.

"You seem to have done well," the secret spy of Treadia murmured. "You sit at the left of the king and he pays more heed to you in the meal than to either his young queen sitting at his right or the visiting dowager queen of Phitio sitting beyond her."

"Yes, I think you could safely say I am positioned much closer to the king than that."

"So I have heard," the spy said and then joined his knowing, low laugh to that of the general's. "I have barely gotten here and it seems I can already return to Treadia with good news."

"Yes, you may do that—and with speed in both returning to Treadia and in setting forth renewed preparation of the warriors of Treadia. You will be hard pressed to start our forces on the move before I will have cut off the head of the four-nations' empire here and thrown Cenopolis and its subservient states into disarray."

"Such good news."

"The speed of the gods send you forth. And as a token of my fealty to our king, please give him this magnificent egg-shaped ruby."

As intent as were the two men in their secret murmurings, they didn't notice the rustling of the tapestry that had covered the hidden door by which the Treadian spy had entered Braxius' chamber, the tapestry held open only enough for the queen dowager of Phitio to hear the gist of what the men were discussing.

As the Treadian spy moved toward the door, the dowager queen withdrew into the labyrinth of passageways tunneled through the walls of the palace and raced to reach her son's chamber before Braxius arrived to debauch him in the night. Her suspicions had been raised by the new, unfamiliar servant in the hall at dinner, and she had followed him, with her eyes while he was in the banquet hall and with her feet when he had stolen away before the servants' work was done. He had been clumsy at serving, which was not tolerated in the king's hall, and he had shown peculiar interest in the person of her son, the king, and the general Braxius. As she padded through the maze of corridors to the king's chambers, she sighed a weary sigh. The labyrinth of life was far more complex than even she had contemplated. A mother's work was never done.

Prophecy of Noto

Chapter One: The Watchman

The Oracle at Noto had prophesized the future glory of high kings arising from Aram. The Watchman himself had made the journey and had returned to tell old King Cresum the news before, even in his moment of joy, the old warrior had given up his own soul to the gods. A progeny of Cresum would rule lands as no other monarch of Aram had and would unify the volatile region of the island of Li' and the civilized rims of dark lands hulking over the island. This prophecy gave the old king the peace he sought before he died. For he had had doubts of his only son, Cletar.

Such a beleaguered nation as Aram required constant and clever care by a strong man, wise in governing. The young prince had shown no interest in the kingship—even now, when his ascension to warrior king was necessary as never before. Instead, he had frittered his youth away with pleasure and debauchery. And even here he had been no use to the line of Cresum, as he was drawn to catamites rather than the king's harem, any woman of which King Cresum would gladly had yielded over to his son—if only his son would provide him with a grandson.

Thus, on the brink not only of the old king's death but also of the advance on the last stronghold of the defending Arameans by the forces of the island king Zara, monarch of the Akamantis on the island of Li', the news from the Oracle at Noto brought through enemy lines, thanks to his protecting cloak of the ancients, by the Watchman, was a voice of salvation.

Only the old king had believed, though. His son, Cletar, had not cared. And the king's own close advisers, the Lord of Sorso and the Lord of Jerzu, as well as the carrion cousins who had gathered around Cresum, ostensibly to give him aid against the Akamantises, but, in reality to be in on the pickings on the king's demise, believed only that the Watchman, the only adviser retained loyalty to the old man to the end, had conjured up the oracle's prophecy, as he conjured up so much else, to soothe the dying man. The strongest of the cousins, Severmist, also known, with much justification as the Prince of Madness, was the most grasping and dangerous, as the size of the sliver of a state he claimed kingship over, Kerastis, did not match the size of his self-esteem and ambition. Nearly equal to him in treachery, was the other cousin in attendance upon King Cresum's death rattle, King Kleemus of Tharsis, the city state that shared the island of Li' with the kingdom of Akamantis.

For the Watchman's part, he did not care what these vultures thought. He knew that oracle had spoken and that he had reported faithfully what it had spoken. And when it had spoken, it gave him strength and assurance—but only to the point of what the oracle added to the prophecy. As he had turned to leave the grotto, he had heard a low laugh and the added phrase, "But only if you make it so."

In contemplating all that had subsequently happened over many years, the Watchman wondered whether the path would have been so much clearer and straight if he had not heard that last phrase—and then done what he did.

And having obtained the oracle's prophecy, the Watchman, who originally had intended to fade into the desert as the false advisers and cousins fought over the leavings of Aram, such as they had become, and dealt with the invading

Akamantis army as they were able, now found that a heavier burden had been assigned to him. He could have let whatever would be come to pass, but the oracle's added dictum had chilled him to the bone. In that instant, he realized that his own fate hung in the balance as well. This had never been part of his existence before. He was of the old ones—one of the last of the ancients. He had served King Cresum's father, and his father, and the father before that. As far as the Watchman could remember, he'd been there at the Creation. But in the one phrase the oracle had uttered, he knew, deep in the heart of him, that if the prophecy did not come about, he too would be finished.

* * * *

It was not even a full changing of the moon since the old king had died and been ascended to the heavens on a flaming pyre at the highest tower of the bastion at Mascus—within sight of the legions of the Akamantis in the valley below—and the Watchman knew this was the crucial night. This was the night that the future the oracle spoke of must be set in motion or the future would collapse into the present and all would be no more than dust and chroniclers' laments.

King Cletar, young and handsome in his dusky, almost womanly beauty, was as much in his cups as usual. The Watchman had stood, in the shadows cast by the torchlight on the stone walls of the king's hall, not wishing to be any part of the travesty he knew was afoot. The king's advisers—Sorso and Jerzu and Severmist and Kleemus—scheming together and separately, had convinced Cletar that the morrow was the most auspicious time to move the army out of the stronghold and engage the enemy in the valley. Cletar was too far into his cups—and anxious to move to his pallet, beyond which the youthful royal catamite, Raum, was already beginning to sway to the music of the flutes, beckoning the young king to join him— to give the venture any thought whatsoever. If his father's advisers and his father's cousins thought this the thing to do, why, then, it must be the thing to do. But that was tomorrow. Cletar had pleasures to pursue tonight.

And so the evening progressed. Cletar approved the attack for the morning and went to the royal pallet, a large pad of many layers of pillows on the floor of the chamber, set before the arches leading out onto the belvedere. Raum was dancing in the moonlight in the belvedere, and the flutists were weaving their soft, musical spells from behind woven hangings at the side of the chamber. From here, upon signal, they could withdraw through a door into a side corridor unseen and unseeing.

Their business finished, all four surreptitiously having exhaustively paired among themselves to weave their individual plots, the advisers' lords and royal cousins gathered around the platform of the king and joined in the enjoyment of the sensuous dance of the talent young catamite. None of the four begrudged Cletar this one last night of life and pleasure, but all were focused on Raum, each with his own dream of owning and enjoying the young dancer when Cletar no longer had use for him—or for anything else in this veil of tears.

As Raum danced, the diaphanous scarves with which he had intriguingly swathed himself began to come off and were languishly cast aside—until he was dancing, his hips sensuously swaying, his full lips humming seductive tune, in only a bejeweled headband and wristbands and ankle bands. Cletar was lying prone on his bier, on his back, besotted and moaning for attention.

The four advisers groaned their need as well, as Raum slowly danced into the chamber from out of the moonlight and circled the platform—the object of the rapt attention of all four advisers as well as the young king. When the dancer mounted the bier, all four drew near, licking their lips and murmuring their anticipation. Raum untied the sash of the king's robes and brushed the material aside, revealing the trembling readiness of Cletar's dusky skin and lean frame. Cletar sighed for the dancing hands of Raum on his ready body, and then there was a heavy release of lustful breath from all sides of the platform, as Raum straddled the king's calves with his knees and moved his hands and mouth to the king's erect phallus.

The Watchman did not see this. He had already withdrawn. He hurried to the harem, knowing that time was crucial to the unfolding of his plan. There he called forth the

Nubian princess Nailah, who was suckling her baby. Not just any harem princess would do, the Watchman knew. He knew that, for his immediate purposes, proven fertility was crucial, and, as strong a warrior as Cresum had been, his reign had taxed his field duties sorely and his harem had been left barren.

Hissing at the woman, he drew her forth. She was frightened to be leaving the harem, but she was not a stupid girl, and she'd known since the death of the old king that she would either be leaving the protection of the harem soon or she would die here, most likely at the piercing cock and sword of some rough, uncouth Akamantis solider. She had every intention of not dying here. She had a son now, and she meant for him to grow to manhood.

In whispers, the Watchman told her of his plan and of her part in it. At first she objected and demurred, but when the Watchman told her that when she had done, he would lead her and her baby to safety, she knew that her salvation had arrived. This was what she had prayed to the gods for. Not deliverance for her, but for her all-important son. Nailah knew of the Watchman and of his powers and of his reputed magical abilities. And she put her faith and future in his hands. Leaving her baby with one of the other woman—for only a short while, the Watchman had promised—she followed him back through the maze of the unknown corridors to behind the woven tapestries in the king's chambers that the flutists had only recently vacated.

Just as the Watchman has hoped—no, as he had willed—the king became thirsty almost immediately after the Watchman had reentered the chamber and taken up a position in the shadow of a stone column. The Watchman closed his eyes and concentrated hard on what needed to pass.

As he wished, the king commanded Raum to take off from his attentions to the royal cock and refill the royal flagon from the table across the room. Although the eyes of all four advisers followed the mincing dancer's progress across the room, the Watchman raised his cloak and, for the briefest moment, neither he nor Raum could be seen—nor did this surprise or concern the four, who returned to whispering among themselves, as the young king belched, and farted, and cried out in a slurred voice the query of why Raum was taking so long.

In the briefest of time, the Watchman told Raum what must happen if he wished to live beyond the setting of the sun on the following day. And Raum, knowing who the Watchman was and of his wisdom, agreed readily to the plan.

When the young dancer returned to the king's bier, he ensured that the king drank of the wine—now augmented with a potion that would keep him awake and in full erection but groggy and unaware after the fact of what had transpired—and Raum mounted the king's pelvis and slid down on his staff and began to move up and down, up and down, in the rhythm of giving and taking and mutual arousing and flow. While he did so, though, he also looked around with smiling and enslaving eyes at the four advisers intently watching him, conveying to each one that this could be them being served thusly by Raum.

When someone spoke, it was Raum, in that honey-rich, seductive tone of his that had ensnared a king-to-be long before he ever had danced on Cletar's cock—offering himself to the four, all at once—and now. The four advisers laughed lustful laughs, each and all seeing and appreciating the joke of depriving the king of this last pleasure—and seizing that pleasure for themselves. In consort, the four reached for Raum and lifted him off the king's cock, each taking possession of a limb of the sensuous dancer, and in a frenzy of wanting, carrying him into a side chamber.

Soon only the king, still moaning, still thinking he was in coitus, was alone in the chamber, save the Watchman and the trembling Nubian princess beyond the tapestries. The sounds from the side chamber told the Watchman in no uncertain terms that the dancer, Raum, was paying heavily for his chance at escape.

"Quick, we must be quick," the Watchman hissed as he drew Nailah from the darkness beyond the tapestry into the torch-lit king's hall.

"I don't know if I can . . ."

"You are a woman; you have done this many times before. This time it will be with one who is young and virile, even though he would not chose to give his seed to a woman. He will not know the difference, however. But the gods will know the difference. And one day Aram will know the difference. I would ask you to do it for Aram, but I know you had no love here beyond the old king. So, you will do it for your own salvation and for that of your own child. And you will be quick about it."

Where Raum had been astride King Cletar's pelvis, Nailah now held sway, working him inside her channel, riding him until he cried out and jerked—and Nailah assured the Watchman that he had spilt his seed.

This was not enough for the Watchman, however. He knew of Cletar's ability—perhaps his one useful talent, not useful to anyone, however, until this moment.

Assured by the not-yet-peaking sounds of the four-cocked taking of Raum from the side chamber, the Watchman made Nailah continue to ride the king's hips as he moaned in his drunken, drugged stupor but yet had the juices to seed the Nubian princess again.

And then the Watchman and Nailah stole back to the harem, where he gave her instructions on where to be at dawn's light and what she could take with her—and that she was to tell no one. Afterward, the Watchman, being no less aroused than the four advisers had been by the dance of Raum, and still very much a man with the ability to stand his phallus, sought out his own catamite, Dila, from the bowels of the stables and took the young stable boy back to his own quarters and rode him until the young man cried for mercy.

* * * *

Shortly after dawn, the Watchman held up his small, motley band—the Nubian princess and her baby, Raum, and Dila—on the upper slopes of Mount Nule, within sight of the stronghold at Mascus and the valley below in time to see the Arameans sally forth from the gates of the stronghold for the all too-short skirmish on the plain below. There in the vanguard was King Cletar, surrounded by his most trusted advisers, those pledged to fight to the death to protect his body and the standard of his throne. Behind them, straggling out of the gates at a leisurely pace, were the ragtag forces of Aram.

The comity of nations dictated that the commanders of the two armies would parley at the middle of the field in a traditional ceremony of forestalling battle if an accommodation could be made. And thus it was this day, with the retinue of the Arameans and that of King Zara of the Akamantis coming together. But in contrast to other times—although, truth be known, not all that uncommon—as the two retinues came together, Cletar's four "faithful" protectors peeled off and rode back to their own, still-forming lines.

"They have left the king alone, defenseless," Nailah cried out, as she hugged her precious baby to her bosom.

"Yes," the Watchman said.

They looked on—three of them in horror, one of them in anticipation of the fulfillment of the inevitable—as King Zara raised his sword and split King Cletar asunder. The young king's stallion rose up on his hind legs, in alarm, and the two pieces of Cletar fell to either side, in the dust of the plain before the gates of Mascus.

But then a nation-saving miracle happened—or so it seemed.

King Zara and his bodyguard, turning away from the rent and bleeding body of the foolish young king of the Arameans, lying in the dust of the plain before his last stronghold, rode their steeds slowly back to the lines of the Akamantis, whereupon the whole enemy army turned its back on Mascus—and trotted into the rising sun. Within the hour, it was as if the siege army had never been there.

"I don't understand," Nailah whispered. "They just left."

"Yes," the Watchman said.

"You are not surprised," Raum said, his honey-rich voice laced with awe. "You knew this is how the day would end."

"Yes," the Watchman conceded. "But I did not have to ask the oracle to know that."

"But who will rule Aram then?" Raum asked.

"The strongest and most treacherous of the four."

"But who is that?"

"It will be King Severmist of the Kerastis, I'm sure," was the answer. "And I don't need a oracle to divine that either. He was the one who made the pact with King Zara of subservience

98

if Zara permitted him to rule Aram. The other three didn't look beyond the possibilities of today. They will be lucky to live to see tomorrow."

"But he is merely a cousin of the old king. He is not a son. Everyone knows that you came back with the message that the oracle said—"

"No, we have the son here," the Watchman said in a steady voice.

And at that, Raum and Dila turned their eyes in the direction in which the Watchman was looking. As all eyes turned to her as she sat astride the donkey, Nailah clutched her baby close to her with one hand and spread her other hand on her belly. And both she and the Watchman knew without a doubt that she was carrying the male child of the dead King Cletar, son of Cresum.

"They will be looking for us, hunting us," Raum said in low, frightened voice.

"Yes, men of many nations will be looking for us—for Nailah—now. So, we must be going."

"But to where?" Dila wailed. "Where can we go that they will not find us?"

"Into the mouth of the lion," the Watchman said.

Raum and Dila each involuntarily emitted a moan. But not the Nubian princess. Nailah just sat on the donkey, clutching the child she already had, her palm resting above the child that was to come, her eyes on the Watchman, trusting him fully and completely.

Chapter Two: The Mouth of the Lion

The Watchman sensed it as it was happening. Such was both the gift and bane the gods had given him—not only that he could see much of what was to come but also that he could sense and feel much of what was happening now beyond his sight. He should have known. Dila was a man and yet he was also a child. When he was a child, as he lay under the Watchman and pleasured the ancient but still-virile rod of his master, this was as the fountain of youthfulness for the Watchman. But Dila also had the mind of a child. Though not devious, he could focus on no more than one aspect of a thought and was petulant. The Watchman had wanted other pleasures for the past three phases of the moon as he taught the dancer, Raum, not only to receive but also to give and to win the hearts and hands of men by doing either, as was necessary.

For the time was close by that a change was necessary. Closer than the Watchman had realized now that his keenest sense honed in on the pouting Dila, who had left their company days before after accusing the Watchman of throwing him over for Raum.

The Watchman was standing on the ridge, the encampment of his companions on one side, down near the sea, on the Gela beach. And on the other side of the ridge the king's high road wound itself around in the undulating hills in the valley. There, along the ridge, at some distance, but not at far enough distance from the Watchman to escape his notice, were Raum and Cleus. Raum, practicing what the Watchman was teaching him, and Cleus . . .

"Oh, Cleus," the Watchman mused. "So much like your father. Too much. And yet there is the spark of your grandfather, the High King Cresum about you as well—and of your mother, Nailah. Not her African beauty. No, most of your beauty you got from your father, the ill-fated Cletar. But you got bravery and persistence—and loyalty—from your mother."

Cleus, a well-muscled dusky god of a man, was lying on his back on a smooth, ridge-top boulder bathed in sunshine, perfectly formed legs held wide and high in the air, while Raum rammed his member with many a snort and grunt between the dark young man's legs, working hard to do Cleus' bidding of reaching new depths, harder rhythms, while Cleus worked his own magnificent staff with his hand.

The vision of Dila was of the unfortunate, foolish young man's last moments under the Sword of Zara. Panting out the shocking, almost amusing, truth that the Watchman had been able to keep secret for just under two decades. Dila, vengeful in his misplaced ire, having left the encampment and sought out the men of Akamantis. Being delivered to the Sword of Zara, the gut-wrenching plowing of which had brought out Dila's assurances that the young prince of the oracle's prophecy did, indeed, live, and then, in his last gasps, as the sword split him asunder, revealing what he had not intended to reveal: where the prince could be found.

The clever truth of the Watchman was now revealed, and from now the significance of time in the lands bordering the Sea of Calm and Storms was beginning again. The rumors, coming first from the harem of Cresum in the stronghold of Mascus— that the Nubian princess not only was missing, but that she also bore a son of Cletar. The fulfillment of the Prophecy of Noto, the promise of which the treacherous advisers of Cletar had tried to nullify by keeping the young king sated with sexual pleasures that could not bear sons.

The Nubian princess and her son of Cletar had been sought for the nearly two decades since then, not only by the Prince of Madness, Cresum's cousin, Severmist, who had grasped control of the kingdom of Aram, albeit not as full king, being under the suzerainty of King Zara of Akamantis; but also by the other cousin, King Kleemus of Tharsis, on the island of Li'; by the two traitorous lords, Soros and Jerzu; and even by— most especially by—King Zara. Of all those threatened, Zara felt threatened the most, as the oracle's prophecy had put his own kingdom under the crown of Cresum's progeny.

All had searched high and low, first in the realm of Aram, and then farther afield: to Mizraim to the west and into— and beyond—Midian in the south into the lands of Cush. And into Meshech and Tubal and even Togarmah in the east. But they never searched under King Zara's own nose—at the edge of the sea on the island of Li', in Zara's own kingdom of Akamantis and almost in the shadow of his own bastion capital of Enna. But this was where the Watchman had taken his precious charges—into the mouth of the lion. And here was where they had been safe until the Watchman's own weakness— his own inability to control and cajole his catamite—was bringing this phase of the Watchman's plan to an end.

The Watchman regretted the circumstance, but he had seen the change coming. And he knew it was time.

Quite possibly his acceptance that it was time and his restlessness to get on with it now that the future had been awakened and set in motion again had nothing to do with the simultaneous materialization of two bands of warriors nearby— or the decision of Raum and Cleus to sink into the mossy dell next to the boulder on the next ridge top, and thus well out of sight, in the throes of their lovemaking was not of the Watchman's making. But then, there also was no more logical explanation of why a raiding party of the Prince of Madness was coming onto shore, headed for and cognizant of the import of the encampment of the Nubian princess, at the same time that a guard unit of Akamantis, in search of what the Sword of Zara had wrenched out of the gasping body of Dila, materialized on the king's high road in the valley below the ridge.

The Watchman had just enough time to glide down from the ridge top and into the back of the princess's tent in time to stay the movement of the princess' first-born son, the diminutive Nubian Toma, from rushing out to the front of the tent to join his mother in standing before the captain of the Aram raiding party.

"Where is he? Where is the son begat on you by King Cletar?"

"There are no king's sons here that you will ever cast your eyes on," Princess Nailah responded haughtily.

"I will find him myself," the captain cried out. And as he moved to brush Nailah aside and enter the tent, she moved also to bar his way.

The time it took to run her through with his sword was enough time for the Watchman to choke off the cry from Toma and swirl his cloak over the youth. When the captain entered the tent, he saw no sons of kings. Cleus was lying in the moss at the top of the ridge, skewered deeply by his dancer lover and oblivious to the action at the seaside. To his eyes, he saw no one at all.

Summoned unexpectedly by a strangled cry from outside the tent, the captain wheeled and staggered out of the tent and into the arms of the Akamantis search party.

The violent, but short, meeting of the forces of Akamantis and Aram on the beach by the sea covered the escape of the Watchman and the Nubian, Toma, to the ridge top, where the pleasures of Raum and Cleus were interrupted, and the companions, one fewer than just minutes before, watched the carnage below.

One of only a few survivors of the Akamantis party would return to Zara with the news that no hidden prince was found, but that he probably existed as the Nubian princess was found—although she unfortunately died in the fighting—and that soldiers of Aram had been on guard in the encampment. The latter information spoke to King Zara, no stranger to duplicitous scheming himself, of the treachery of his vassal, the Prince of Madness. And this was the basis of renewed open hostilities between the two kingdoms. None of the raiding party of Aram returned to the stronghold of Mascus alive, though. And thus Severmist, the Prince of Madness, could only guess at why the heads of his diplomats in the court of King Zara were returned to him without their bodies and the hostilities of the two kingdoms facing each other, almost in sight of one another, across a narrow stretch of the Sea and Calm and Storms had resumed. He chose to believe that the rumors that the royal son of the Prophecy of Noto existed and was being succored in the kingdom of Zara were true. And he began to plan a full invasion, mindless of the years it would take to bring to pass, commencing with the building of a massive fleet and training of an army in secret. He knew that King Zara did not believe he had the resources for such an undertaking ever.

Back on the seaside beach, Cleus was standing over the grave of his mother, arm and arm with his lover, Raum, and flanked by his half brother, Toma, and his sole adviser, the Watchman.

The Watchman looked at the two near brothers, Cleus and Toma. They could not be more unalike. Cleus was tall and strong, and beautifully muscled. His appearance was dusky, but not Nubian. Toma, on the other hand, was small and, while still well formed, was willowy and childlike—and mistakenly was a child of Africa. Thinking of what he had foolishly lost—the couplings with Dila—and looking at Toma, similar of stature and demeanor to Dila, the Watchman's juices began to flow. Dare he? Would the gods strike him dead? Well, if they did, it

103

would take this burden off his shoulders of seeing that the Prophecy of Noto came to pass.

"What do we do now?" Cleus asked, with a weary sadness in his voice. "We cannot stay here. Others will follow these."

"And what of Maia?" Toma asked.

A good sign of Toma's basic character, the Watchman thought, as he looked down at the young, alluring Nubian, trying to hide in his eyes the lust he felt in his body. Toma had thought of the young maiden in the village on the other side of the ridge, the woman Toma had been lying with for some months.

"Do I tell him she is with child—and that it is a son?" the Watchman asked himself. "But then he thought it not wise. But it was a good thing for he himself to know. A very good thing indeed."

"We must endure even more hardships now than before," the Watchman said, trying to couch his voice in regret, although, now that it was happening, he was anxious to get back onto the journey of the fulfillment of the prophecy. "If you truly love your Maia, Toma, do you want to put her through those trials?"

Toma thought hard, and the Watchman thought that the tears forming at the corner of his eyes were a charming aspect of the young man who was stirring him inside so now.

"No. No, I suppose not," Toma answered at length. "But the thought of never seeing her again—"

"You will see her again," Toma. "I promise you that. You will be with Maia again. She could not be safer anywhere else."

The Watchman looked with a love of his own into the eyes of what was now his conquest. What he said was true, but only he knew how hard the road would be for Toma from this time to that.

Toma looked back into the Watchman's eyes with awe, gratitude, and acceptance. But he also saw something else— something both frightening and arousing.

"But where will we go?" Cleus repeated.

"We have been safe in the mouth of the lion for some time. We will go into the mouth of another lion."

"Back to Aram. To the court of the Prince of Madness?" Raum asked, being the first one to discern the Watchman's meaning.

"Yes," was the Watchman's simple answer.

"But how can we do that? Won't we be—?" Cleus murmured.

"In the court at Mascus, only Raum and I are known," the Watchman answered. "I can take many forms and still be nearby. But Raum is known—and was accepted—at court. There was no hint that he left with us—is with us. He was in high favor in the minds and bodies of Severmist and the others. Their one night with him will have been magnified in their minds as a heaven worth pursuing and preserving. He will be welcome back with open arms and erect staffs."

"That is fine for me," Raum answered. "But Cleus and Toma?"

"Both are beautiful, desirable young men. You already have Cleus in training. The court will be delighted for you to bring willing and accomplished protégés with you when you return."

"Yes, I can see that. But Toma?"

"Toma I will train myself," the Watchman answered simply and in a tone that permitted demur by no one there—including Toma. Nor did Toma, still wondering over what he had seen in the Watchman's eyes, whisper a word of objection.

And later that night, as he lay on his back with the Watchman hovering over him, and his robe was gently split aside and the Watchman's hands seemed to be everywhere—on his chest; between his thighs; cradling his head; as the Watchman brought lips down to his; encasing his ball sack; squeezing his cock; fingers entering his channel—and then crying out in the pain-pleasure of the Watchman entering him deeply and oh so strongly for an ancient and beginning to churn inside him, Toma learned what was meant by the Watchman training him himself.

And there, in the night, his prodigious staff pinning the lithe, small body of the Nubian youth to the moss of the ground at the top of the ridge, the gods answered the one concern the Watchman had had and assured him that he was on the right path. Lying there, amazed, his monster of a cock all inside the small young man and yet Toma moaning and panting from pleasure now rather than unconscious from splitting, the Nubian's channel walls yielding and opening to the Watchman, the Watchmen felt his member growing—lengthening and thickening beyond all arousals of his earlier centuries. And has his cock grew—from a dirk to a rapier to a broad sword to a pike to a veritable ancient cypress-tree trunk from the forests of Phoenicia, the Nubian's channel continued to open and widen for him. The cock head must be in the belly now and probing on for yet another channel. And still the Nubian stayed with him, panting and moaning and moving his hips in a wave-like motion. The muscles of his channel walls undulating over the Watchman's inhumanly proportioned staff.

Until the Watchman was lost in the taking, riding the waves of a tumultuous sea, flowing his seed in strong bursts—once, twice, thrice, four times—being milked as never before. Never wanting it to stop; never wanting to be outside his Nubian lover again.

In awe, lying there at the end, the Nubian gently snuffling in sleep in the crook of his arm, the Watchman had no doubt that this was serving the Prophecy of Noto. That he had not presumed too much. That the gods were opening the path to him. He knew know exactly what would happen—what he had to do. And how the prophecy was to be fulfilled. He had done no damage in his earlier stumbling in the dark and his own attempts to serve the prophecy. But neither was he smarter than the oracle.

Chapter Three: The Sword of Zara

"I think it's wreckage of a ship. From the storm last night." It wasn't strange to find ship wreckage on the Cefalu beach, in the kingdom of Akamantis, after a tempest like had raged the previous night.

Two scouts, on their regular patrol along the coastline of the island of Li' in vigilance against the forces of the Prince of Madness, which sought to invade Akamantis, had stopped on the beach, their attention arrested by shattered ship planking and tangles of shredded sailcloth washing up in the surf.

"Shall we hope that it is a ship of the Aram, even perhaps the flagship of the old mad prince himself?" said the second of the scouts, as they pulled up their horses on the cliff above the beach.

This particular beach had been scouted constantly over the past few weeks, because twice the Oracle at Noto had said the invasion would come here, on the beach at Cefalu. If it spoke the same name the third time, this would be a certainty.

"What ho?" called out the first scout. "I see movement below, in the wreckage."

The two spurred their horses along the cliff front until they came to the winding path that led down the beach.

As they approached, a figure was pulling his way out of a pile of splintered timbers. He was slight, but well formed, and brown as the earth in the fields of Li'. No, he was browner, a rich chocolate brown. And he had black curly hair and was handsome of face and limb. As he stumbled to stand and the two riders drew nearer, they could see that his clothes, typical in style and color of the hated Aram ruling family, were in tatters.

The first rider unsheathed his short lance, ready to erase one more Aramean from the earth, but the other stayed his hand.

"Nay, brother, can you not see? He is one of the browns, one of those we call the Nubians. Not a real Aramean."

"Yet he wears the vestments of the Aram and no doubt is part of the invasion fleet. He should be dispatched."

"No, hold," the second scout called out again. "Have you not heard? Have you not heard that the browns are meant for the Sword of Zara? The Sword of Zara hungers for them, and this one appears to be well formed. We will take him back to Enna, to the Sword of Zara. The Sword of Zara will dispatch the lad. This too may be an omen, a favorable omen. We will be rewarded."

The small Nubian man had come to his senses enough to see the two horsemen bearing down on him, in the livery of King Zara. And in apparent panic he turned from them and stumbled as in confusion and exhaustion across the burning sands on naked feet.

It was a futile gesture. The two scouts bore down on him, and the first scout reached down and lifted the small young man easily and slung him, belly down in front of him, on the back of the horse. Anxious now to pass on the treasure they'd found, the scouts turned the noses of their mounts toward the land and raced up the sand and across the dunes to the king's high road.

If they had been more observant and in less of a hurry, they might have looked back to where the young Nubian had risen from out of the wreckage of the ship and seen a second figure, a wizened old man, bent over and stumbling into the brilliant sunlight—and lifting his head to watch the horses disappearing over the rise of the dunes . . . and forming a smile, a pleased little smile, on his lips.

The two scouts were cantering back toward the capital of Enna when a large contingent of horseman approached from the central plains at a gallop.

The first scout, recognizing the horsemen of the king, raised himself up in the saddle and waved his lance back and forth, signaling that they had news. By the time the larger force had drawn up before them, the two scouts were off their horses and on their knees, heads bowed.

From out of the pack of horseman emerged a man taller and bulkier and more majestic than all of the rest. He strode to where the two scouts were kneeling, their eyes cast to the ground, their shoulders trembling as all men in the kingdom trembled in the presence of their king.

"Why do you impede my progress?" the king growled. "Are you not supposed to be on coastal watch? What have you seen? And it better not be a trifle."

"No, my lord, it is no trifling matter," the first scout replied in a shaky voice. "We have seen wreckage, the wreckage of a ship, perhaps an Aram warship, on the beach at Cefalu. As the oracle said—"

"I know what the oracle said," thundered the king. "I speak to the oracle. Only I. I do not expect my scouts to speculate on what they do not know. The storm of last night was mighty. It may have been one of our ships."

"Beg your mercy, lord," the second scout ventured, "But there is evidence."

"Evidence? What evidence? Evidence of what?"

"We have found a survivor. The tatters of his clothes are in Aram style and color. And, you will be pleased to know—"

"Don't tell me what will please me. Did you leave the body on the beach?"

"No, sire," offered the first scout. "He is here, on my horse. We spared him because we understand the likes of him are for the Sword of Zara. He is African brown."

"The Sword? A Nubian?" The king was suddenly interested. "Let me see this one?"

The first scout popped up and dragged the Nubian captive off his horse and set him on the ground, but so weak was the survivor of the shipwreck that he sank to the ground on his knees.

The eyes of the king lit up, and he smiled broadly and stood his full stature. The muscles on his chest seemed to expand, and he became a god of men, a man of huge and divinely sculpted countenance.

"A sign. Another sign beyond the pronouncement of the oracle that we are to look to the Cefalu beach for invasion," the king announced in a voice that rung out over the gathered contingent.

"Yes, this is one for the Sword." the king declared. "To be dispatched by the Sword of Zara. And on the altar. We are near the hill of the altar to the sea. Come bring him to me there."

The scouts took up the trembling Nubian captive and slung him on the horse's back once more. Then they merged their steeds in with those of the king's contingent, their minds trying to form the reward that would be theirs for this day's work, and the force moved up to the top of a hill overlooking the sea. Here there was a small, low-lying altar of smooth stone, flat, with horns of bulls wedged at the corners.

At the king's direction, the Nubian was pulled off the horse, and his tattered clothing was stripped completely away.

He was laid on his back on the altar, and his wrists were tied with a leather thong and forced over his head and attached loosely to the horns at corners above his head.

His eyes were wide in fright, and he was mumbling his fear and begging for mercy in the universal language of the kingly classes. All the men gathered around him in awe. A Nubian knowing the universal language and one of such delicate but well-formed beauty. Taken for a child at first, he had the stubbling on his chin that revealed him to be older. His figure was trim, but he was well muscled and smooth skinned, with no callusing. He was no normal Nubian servant. He was someone special to someone of the royal court of Aram. His cock and balls were those of a youth, but they were in excellent proportion to his body. He had the beauty of an ebony statue.

"You are not of low estate, are you?" The king demanded, as he walked through the circle of men and stood tall and mighty at the base of the altar. "Tell me who your master is."

The Nubian did not answer. He went silent and just lay there, trembling.

"Right. You will talk while you live," the king bellowed. "But now the Sword of Zara wants you. You will talk before the might of the Sword. Tell me what I want to hear and I will dispatch you quickly. Otherwise I will tear you to shreds from the inside."

All grew silent on the sacred mound, all except for the panting and involuntary whimpering of the Nubian captive, no longer speaking, having already betrayed himself as an educated man.

Knowing the ritual as they did and the Nubian did not, the onlookers knew the king was toying with the young man. The Sword of Zara would tear him to shreds anyway. They groaned and moaned in chorus in anticipation of the entertainment.

The king held out his arms, which had the span of an oak. And when he did so, men pressed forward at the crouch and unlaced his armor. They lifted it off his magnificent torso and did as well with his tunic and backed away, the one holding the kingly garment of linen shot through with threads of gold folding it reverently in his arms.

The king stood there in only his short skirt and his sandals that laced up his calves in ropes of gold. When the attendants had unlaced and taken away the strips of metal that had hung down from the golden belt at his waist, his only remaining adornments were gold bands on his biceps and high on his thighs, the one on his right thigh holding the sheath for a golden dirk knife. The king was old by the standards of the day, but he was of excellent stock and was in battle trim.

The king himself reached to the small of his back and unlaced the waistband of his short skirt.

"I am King Zara," he bellowed to the heavens, "and this," he declared in a ring tone, "is the Sword of Zara." At that he dropped his short skirt and all in attendance, not the least the Nubian captive lying on the altar, gasped at the revealing of the longest, thickest cock on the island nation of Akamantis. Hanging down behind the huge cock was a set of matching balls the size of cannon balls.

"Prepare!" the king declared, and three attendants shot forward and took turns working the king's cock with their mouths and rubbing it with ointment.

Two other attendants surged forward and grabbed the Nubian captive by his ankles, one on each side, and pulled his body down to where his perfectly rounded buttocks were on the edge of the altar top. And then they lifted and spread his legs out, rolling his pelvis up to receive the Sword.

No one present, including the king, thought that the sheathing of the Sword was going to be possible; they all assumed that the Nubian would expire at the first thrust. Still, they knew that even in death the Sword would be thrust inside— and would continue its thrusting until the king's seed had been split—and the sacrifice would be torn asunder and lose his lifeblood at the base of the altar. All took a step forward, licking lips, anxious for the rarely seen spectacle, wanting to see the expression on the Nubian's face and hear his last strangled yowl as the thrust of the Sword transmitted him to the world of the dead.

Everyone looked at the king, now in full erection, and saw that his cock was as long and thick as the Nubian captive's forearm.

This was what the Akamantises did with any stray brown person finding himself on the island. The customs were ancient and clear. The brown people—the Nubians—were a sign of good luck for the island. But only if they were dispatched with the sword of the ruling king. No king in history had had the sword that King Zara possessed. Thrice before Nubians had been brought to him during his reign. And each time good times had come to Akamantis when he had dispatched the Nubian with his sword. Only one had survived the first thrust, and then only for a matter of moments. A Nubian like this was a sign of the Oracle at Noto and a gift from the gods.

And this was the smallest Nubian sacrifice of all. All attention was on the altar, no one wanting to miss anything, titillated at the image to come of a giant taking a dwarf, and all assuming it would be an entertainment of but a moment's length before all of the life would be out of the screaming dwarf.

The king approached the Nubian between his spread legs. He unsheathed his golden dirk and placed the tip under the chin of the young man. Looking down at the Nubian, the king was in full arousal. The captive was pure beauty, the height of sensuality to the king. He would not make this quick if he could help it. He did not relish dispatching the arousing young man as quickly as the others. But even in death, the king would have his sheathing and plant his seed at the center of the Nubian.

The king placed the huge bulb of his monstrous cock at the hole of the Nubian and leaned over and looked closely into the young man's face.

"Tell me who you are and who you serve and how you came to be on the beach of my kingdom," the king growled.

"I am Toma," the young man murmured. "And I serve the gods. Beyond that I cannot say. Kill me if you wish. I cannot say."

The king watched with relish as his bulb gained purchase in the young captive's hole, which caused the Nubian to shudder and his head to veer back and his howl of pain and stretching to be cried to the heavens. The king was pleased with the expression on the captive's face; it made the king feel mighty and invincible.

"The heavens cannot help you, little one," the king muttered. "The heavens favor me, and you have been sent as yet another favorable sign. Now, tell me, who do you serve and how do you come to be on my beach? It will go quickly with you if you tell me now. Slowly if you tell me later. But tell me, you will."

Silence.

The king, angry now, pushed his greased member in several inches in one thrust. The pupils rolled back into the eyes of the Nubian captive, and he screamed a scream that stopped in mid voicing, and he had passed out.

All in attendance thought he was dead, indeed thought that the taking he had received was enough for him to be dead, but the king saw that the young man still breathed, in shallow breaths, and he signaled attendants, who stepped up and slapped the captive on the face until he was revived.

"Who do you serve and how do you come to be on my beach?"

The Nubian just looked the king steadily in the eye and was silent.

Angry again, the king started to thrust even farther into the channel of the youth, but now it was he who gasped. The surprise was his now, as the Nubian's channel expanded, and the undulating muscles of his canal seized the king's cock and pulled him deep, deep, relentlessly deep into the center of the Nubian captive. And then the young man arched his back and raised his pelvis further. He jerked his ankles out of the grasp of the attendants and crossed his legs tightly above the king's buttocks and started to fuck the king in a steady rhythm, a rhythm involuntarily taken up by the loins of the king—the Nubian captive, not the king, in control of the fuck.

The shocked king was lost in ever greater waves of arousal. He dropped his dirk, and when the Nubian raised his lips to the king's, they went into a deep sensual kiss.

The king was lost in full fuck now, forgetting tradition and custom and the sacrifice completely. And the flowing he experienced was the best he'd had in memory.

Afterward he collapsed on top of the breast of the Nubian, and Toma put his lips to the ear of the king and murmured, "I serve you, if you will have me. And I came to be on the beach because the gods sent me to endure the sheathing of the Sword of Zara and to pleasure the king of the Akamantises for as long as you will have me."

Recovered, the king bluffed for all of his warriors in attendance to hear by declaring in a voice he tried to make as ringing as possible following the complete draining of his manhood by this little one that the gods had sent the Nubian Toma to answer to the arrogance of the Aram and that he would be locked away in the castle to be sacrificed on the altar of the sun there, the altar of the sea not being worthy enough for this sacrifice.

The gathered crowd murmured in awe, knowing that the altar of the sun was so sacred that only the king could approach it.

And so, Toma was locked away in the king's chambers and in due time the king issued the announcement that he had been sent to the gods on the altar of the sun. King Severmist was still faced with the dilemma of who this Nubian was. The first time the king called for Toma, however, Toma straightaway gave the king the answers he had originally sought.

"I will keep no secrets from you, my lord, as long as you search my depths with the Sword of Zara. Only you have brought me satisfaction. Before coming to you, I served the Lord of Sorso, who was lost at sea that stormy night, he along with all of his forces. Only I survived, being sent to you by the gods to serve you. And I gladly tell you that it is more than the forces of the Lord of Sorso who are no longer with the prince who besieges you. The Lord of Jerzu has deserted him as well, with all of his contingent. And the puss sickness has taken away even some of the prince's forces. But it is true, he is the Prince of Madness. He insists on attacking you and taking Akamantis. He knows you do not have the forces to cover all of the approaches to your island kingdom. He believes he can find your unprotected underbelly."

"He does not know what I know, little one," King Zara said. He was laying on his bed of pillows, holding the small

Toma to him and running his hands over the Nubian's body. He was transported by the brown bodies of the Nubians. He had regretted the short play time he had had with the first three sent to him. He had no idea how this young man had managed him on the altar, although he had only been half sheathed when he had given up his seed in surprise. Toma was arousing him to the heights, but he did not want to kill the young man with his sword until he had learned more from him. In the meantime, he was toying with Toma's hole with his thumb, which was larger in itself than the cocks of most Akamantises, and Akamantis men were famous for their thick cocking.

Toma was sighing and began to move his hips on King Zara's thumb and, without thinking about it, the king had substituted first one and then two fingers.

"He does not know that we know precisely where he will land. The Oracle at Noto has told us so. It has spoken twice. When it speaks the same name the third time, we will know for sure, and that is where we will position our defenses."

"I fear for you, my king," Toma said, as he reached down and held the wrist of the hand the king was slowly finger fucking him with. The king felt the pull of Toma's channel upon his fingers, and he inserted another one.

"You are being led astray. I cannot remain silent. I must prove myself to you. I yearn for your sword, which reached farther into me than any other man's ever has. Please I beseech you, sheath your sword in me once more, and then I will tell you secrets that will shake you to your very soul."

"I do not want to dispatch you," the king murmured. "I wish to play with you further. But I am too much for you. You cannot survive me."

"Nay, sire," Toma said. And then he laughed. "Look, sire, look for your hand."

The king looked down at the hand he was using to play with Toma's hole and gasped in shock. His whole hand up to his wrist was inside Toma now, and yet Toma's channel muscles were working to pull his arm even deeper.

The king's lust knew no bounds, and he rose and, with effort, pulled his fist from out of the Nubian's ass and lifted the young man up with broad hands more than encircling his waist and settled Toma's hole over his fully erect sword.

"At least I feel I must lap you," the king said, "lest I crush your body. That at least is too delicate for my frame."

The king pulled Toma half way down on his cock and began to lift him and bring him down, beginning the rhythm of the fuck.

After the initial cry and groan, Toma began to pant and moan. "Nay, my king. Sheath your sword in its entirety. I must have it all."

To the king's amazement, Toma did take it all. The king had never fully sheathed his sword; he had killed many a wife and concubine trying to do so. And after the king had given over his seed, Toma refused to release him, clamping down his channel muscles tight and demanding a second ride and then a third—until the king, virile as he was, had no more kingly seed to give, no more power in his pelvis and thigh and buttocks muscles, and just lay back, exhausted and sighing the satisfaction of total fulfillment.

Toma slithered up to where his lips were at the ear of the king.

But the king spoke first. "You are no innocent young man; you are a king's catamite, are you not?"

"Yes, lord, Toma answered in a whisper. I was the Lord of Sorso's catamite, but he did not satisfy me, and then the Lord of Jerzu's, and he did not satisfy me. And then both lords at once, and still they did not satisfy me. Three men have I taken at once, and still I was not touched to the quick. I went to the prince, and he did not satisfy me. But I satisfied him, and he confided in me. And I had heard about you and that you had the most magnificent member in all the world. And so I came to you. And you satisfy me, my lord. You, today, have reached me to the very center—not once but three times. You are an elephant of men."

They kissed, the king's vanity stroked to the limit, lost in love, blind to love and his Nubian lover from this point forward.

"And in your satisfying of me, I must tell you all. I must whisper it in your ear as even the walls of your palace have ears and tongues that speak to the Prince of Madness. You must not

116

believe in your oracle. The Prince of Madness has suborned your oracle. It is not the beach at Cefalu where the attack will occur. It is the beach of Gela, on the other side of the island. You must gather your forces there."

"But the oracle—"

"Bought and paid for by the Prince of Madness, who is not really that. He is really the Prince of Darkness. I know as no other man does. His cock is as long as yours, but it is not as thick. It is not an honest sword. It is a serpent's tongue, hissing and slithering inside me. And it is as black as his heart. I cannot let this prince prevail over you. That is why I have come to you."

"But I go to the oracle tomorrow."

"No matter what it says, you must announce the truth and prepare for war in the right place. But now you must sheath your sword inside me once again. The very quick of me wants to feel the prick of your blade tip."

The cries and sighs and moans emitted by Toma during this fourth cocking assured the king that he satisfied his Nubian lover in each successive sheathing more than the previous one.

The next day King Zara made the last of three ceremonial visits to the oracle. And, sure enough, the word that was whispered and echoed all around the smoky cave walls was "Cefalu."

"It repeated 'Cefalu' for the third time, but, even as you say, I think I could hear the treachery in its voice," the king whispered to his new catamite when he returned from visiting the oracle in private so that his court did not know the consultations were finished and they were alone inside the canopy of the king's bed. "But the more I think on it, the more I hear the true oracle whispering the name of the beach at Gela to me. This is not the first I have heard of the beach. This is where the little Aramean lad who came to me told me of the presence of prince of the oracle as well as where the prince could be found—but who was not there when my men searched him out. Yes, that makes sense. But what can I do?" the king moaned into Toma's ear as he cuddled the Nubian into his belly and entered him deeply. "I certainly cannot tell my people that my Nubian lover has told me the Oracle at Noto lies. They would pull me apart limb from limb and feed me to the Galotes. I am not

117

mighty enough to withstand all of the men who would align against me. And they think you are dead, anyway, sacrificed on the altar of the sun."

"There is no problem, King," Toma whispered in the king's ear as he pushed the king on his back and straddled his hips and began his own soothing ritual once more. "You go alone to the cave, saying this is the final consultation. Merely say that you went in and the name whispered was 'Gela.' And that as you were leaving the cave in confusion, the oracle called you back—twice—and the name 'Gela' echoed each time, providing the three declarations that told you the truth."

"I don't know. I . . . Oh . . . my ancestors!" Toma had descended full way on the Sword of Zara and was sheathing and unsheathing it and melting away all of the king's concerns and reason.

On the day of his departure, as the king was putting on his armament before leaving the palace at Enna, Toma came to him, a dirk hidden in the lining of his robe. "Let me go with you, King Zara. Let me show my loyalty and pledge of truth by riding with you."

"No, little one," the king replied. "You ride with me as far as the village of Favara, in heavy disguise, but no further than that. You are unknown in my world, having already been thought to have been sacrificed to the Sword of Zara on the altar of the sun. I cannot give you up, but neither can I display you. And I cannot trust those I am leaving here to protect you. It's a simple village, but they are my kinsmen, and they will give you sanctuary. There will be no guards, no sign that the king's most precious treasure resides there."

Toma secretly rejoiced at the naming of the village of Favara, for he already knew there was a treasure there—nay, two treasures. And, although he fingered his hidden dirk, he knew now that the Watchman had told him true—that, although what he did would lead to the removal for all time of King Zara, it would not be Toma's hand that did the dispatching. Strangely enough, the Watchman had said that Toma had other, far more valuable talents and gifts than that of a warrior.

On the day of the invasion of the kingdom of Akamantis on the island of Li', in the month that Akamantis came under the sway of the country of Aram, Toma was standing tall on the cliff overlooking the beach at Cefalu to welcome the arrival of his sovereign and lover, the Prince of Madness, and a mighty force that included the contingents of the Lords of Sorso and Jerzu. In far off Enna, the allied forces were already inside the walls of the capital before the army King Zara had arrogantly and secretly sent forth to the beach as he himself returned to the comfort of his palace, even realized that they had been duped by a small Nubian spy with a talent fit for a king.

Transporting back to Enna on the winds of the Watchman's magic, Toma was set down on the top of the breached bastion wall in time to see the figure of his half brother, Cleus, at the forefront of the fighting, slashing his way into the inner circle of King Zara's defenses. The Nubian's heart leaped with joy at each avenging thrust from Cleus' sword into the heart of the traitorous murderer of his father, Cletar.

Standing beside him, a wizened, bent old man in a dark brown cloak laid a trembling hand on arm of the small Nubian he had trained ever so well. "Have you had your fill of the sight of the Aram forces, my son? Do you not wish to return now to Favara—to the arms of your wife, Maia, and of your own young son?"

"Yes, I am ready, Watchman," Toma murmured. "But what of you? And how does this help our goals for the Prince of Madness to hold sway in Akamantis as well as Aram?"

"All in good time, my son. You have done well; this is all according to plan. I remain in Enna for now. There is much more that is to be done."

"And so we part here? I have done my part?"

"We part here for now, yes. But as far as doing your part, no, my son, it will seem to you someday that your part had not even started at this point. And we will surely meet again. In Enna."

Chapter Four: The Tharsisian Horse

Old King Severmist of Kerastis, Aram, and Akamantis stood on a rock outcropping on the seaside of the pass through the Golden Mountains down into the rich plains of Tharsis and shook his fists in frustration and despair. For the third time in as many days the frontal assault on the High Castle of King Kleemus, his cousin and erstwhile ally, had failed.

"How much longer will you hold against my might?" the old king roared out in his obsession. "Two long years. See this beard? It nigh reaches the ground and is as gray as the skies over your winter land."

"Perhaps it is time to suggest just going around the castle and down into the valley, sire," one of the king's advisers said timidly, cowering at the king's side. Unfortunately, he had come too close, though, and, with one swipe of his mail-encased hand, the king slapped him across the path, from whence he did not rise.

The king knew they could not continue this siege for two more years. His own health would not permit it. He would not live to enter Tharsis then, and all would be lost without him at the helm. Then his mission would be frustrated—to seal his legitimacy even after his death and put to rest for all time the ebbing rumor of the Oracle at Noto's declaration of high kingship over all of the lands in the region for the progeny of old King Cresum.

"The high castle remains the key," he growled. "It is the strongest point in Tharsis. If we take the castle, all of the rest in the valley will open their doors to us. If not, it is a fight on every doorstep and a lance at our backs, between us and the sea. We must have the castle. Must I do the thinking for us all? Is there no one here with the wit to follow on from me?"

"Sire," a low, but assured voice spoke up from the shadows, "Might I—?"

"Why be you here?" the king cried out, almost in anguish. "You are nothing but the king's dancer and the sheath for my sword. You belong in the train with the women and the other women in men's clothes. How dare you attend and speak out. Better yet, get you to the High Castle. From what is reported to me, those within are sodomites all."

"We have Raum in the castle." Cleus gritted his teeth at the arrogance and convenient memory of Severmist. Where was he, Cleus thought, when I led the storming of Enna. He was sipping in his cups on his flagship off the beach at Cefalu, Cleus added in his mind, supplying his own answer. He was determined to continue in the forefront of this siege, though, and to show his metal to all those who would survive Severmist. He, continued with his counsel, "Perhaps we—"

"Be damned and be gone with you, pup. It is because of you that Raum is there. I'll have no more words from you, boy."

And then all was silent as the shadows of night descended on the pass from the sea through the Golden Mountains and down into Tharsis, and the lights in the High Castle yet burned, telling of comfort and safety.

And yet the king's catamite was so bold to have not returned to Enna as summoned. He knew the old king—the man he'd known as the Prince of Madness—was mercurial and would call for him in the night, not remembering he had been dismissed, and roaring with anger if he were not there.

And sure enough, the many moldering war wounds and advance of age in King Severmist's body were denying him sleep and he called for his calamite. And the young man was there in an instant, naked and bearing the soothing oil with which he rubbed his king's body before taking the old man's phallus in his mouth and bringing him to life and then straddling him and riding his staff like a camel in the Aram desert until the old man dribbled his seed and drifted off to sleep with no more than a murmured, "Thank you, Cleus."

From the shadows, the Watchman kept vigil. He could end it now for the traitor to his own king with the sigh of a dirk. But this fulfillment of the prophecy of the oracle needed to be public. The prophecy was fading. It needed to be brought to life in a way that all could see and there would be no doubt, no hesitation for all to bow their knee.

As he had planned many years ago, Cleus would be the vehicle for this part of what needed to be.

* * * *

The Grand Marshal of Tharsis, the man closest to King Kleemus and his principal military adviser, the man who had devised and carried out the successful defense of Tharsis against the invading barbarians from the sea in close consort with his king for the past two years, was galloping through the forest at the valley base of the High Castle with his small band of hunters, bringing home venison. The Grand Marshal distained the forces of the Akamantis and went out on these forays on purpose to show those under siege in the High Castle how safe they were in his hands. Few raiding parties ventured beyond the castle and down into the valley, and the Grand Marshal's spies knew when they were afoot.

But on the road to the castle, the Grand Marshal pulled his horse up and his lip curled up. Here was something he had not been apprised of. Heads would roll for overlooking this.

Off on the side of the trail he spied a gypsy wagon, turned on its side, its contents strewn out around it and obviously the subject of pillage.

The Grand Marshal trotted over to the wagon, its scarlet and yellow wheels still spinning, and reached down and jerked an arrow out of the undercarriage and lifted it up for all to see.

"Double-edged point," said one minion.

"Red feather," said another.

"An arrow of the Akamantis," chimed in a third.

The Grand Marshal nodded his head in grim agreement. The forces of the Akamantis and of their new king, Severmist of Aram, were becoming bolder. They were foraying too far into the valley. And his spies had missed this intrusion.

All of the riders were startled by the sound of a groan—coming from under the upturned wagon. Quick as a dart, two of the minions dismounted and, with all of their strength, lifted the wagon, and a third pulled out the body of a young man.

The rescuer turned him over on his back, and the Grand Marshal's heart leaped in his chest and his cock stood at immediate attention.

The young man was beautifully built and provocatively displayed. He was a dusky beauty, and with an athlete's build—

but dressed as a dancer—one of the rare firmly muscled, well-worked dancer's bodies, with every part perfectly formed. The Grand Marshall liked fucking men, not effeminate boys. And if the man were trained to the dance and the art of seduction, all the better. The young man had an achingly beautiful face, with full, sensuous lips and short, tightly curled hair most often seen in Nubians but quite fetching in a youth as handsome as this. He was nearly naked, stripped to the waist, gold belted, and wearing diaphanous, billowing pantaloons of some white material shot through with threads of gold. He had gold snake bracelets encircling his biceps and gold rings in his nipples, and, as could clearly be seen, a gold ring in the bulb of his cock as well. These all were the markings of a catamite, one whose purpose in life was to sheath a man's cock.

"Does he live?" The Grand Marshal asked in a strained voice, and upon hearing an assent, he dismounted and moved in one graceful, fluid motion to where the young man lay.

"Lay him on the carriage body," he commanded, and the young man was lifted and laid on his back on the edge of the carriage.

The Grand Marshal withdrew his dirk knife and gathered up the flimsy material of the young man's pantaloons at the crotch in one fist and slit through the material with the knife he held in the other hand. Sheathing his knife, he spread the young man's legs with hands fisting his ankles.

With the first strong thrust of his engorged cock in the young man's channel, the youth's obsidian-black eyes opened in shock and he cried out in the taking. "Oh, oh, Lord. Nay, please I beg you. I have never . . . Oh, no, I am undone." His cries turned to moans and groans, as the Grand Marshal's minions just stood about, looking at the ground—when they weren't stealing furtive looks at the taking of the young man. No one raised a hand to stay the Grand Marshal. He was the second-most powerful man in the land, his blood and lust ran hot, and—save for deference to King Kleemus himself—he took his pleasures when and with whom he would, whether or not they were willing.

The young dusky god's cries of undoing changed in short order to cries for the fuck. He arched his back and raised his pelvis and started meeting the Grand Marshal's relentless thrustings with counterthrusts of his own. He cried out of the Grand Marshal's artistry and mastery of the cocking and of how he'd never known it could be like this and how much he loved the movement of the Grand Marshal's superior member deep inside him. He writhed and trembled and shuddered beneath the onslaught of the old warrior, and his hands reached out and caressed the thick matting of hair on the Grand Marshal's chest and reached up and palmed the back of the old warrior's neck and brought his face down to his and opened his sweet lips to the invasion of the Grand Marshal's tongue.

Not long before the Grand Marshal experienced the longest and strongest ejaculation of his recent memory, the young god had given up his own seed with the rubbing of his gold-ringed cock head on the old man's still-hard belly.

By the time the climax ensued, an objective observer would be hard pressed to suppose just who had fucked who—and the Grand Marshal was hopelessly smitten.

The young man, Cleus by name, and, by his own declaration, a wandering musician and dancer by trade, was taken up to the castle and installed in the Grand Marshal's apartments, where the Grand Marshal became besotted with watching him dance and then fucking him day and night until it became clear to King Kleemus that he was not being as fully attended as he once had been by his principal adviser. This did not necessarily set well with the king.

The king was not the only one who had taken notice of this change in circumstance. His young attendant and sometimes lover, Raum, known to Kleemus since the days of King Cresum's court in Aram's principle stronghold of Mascus, had also heard rumors of the young, enticing god living in the Grand Marshal's apartments, a handsome, dusky young dancer with obsidian-black eyes; full, sensuous lips; and golden rings at the nipples and cock head. Raum knew of only one person in the world who met this description. He therefore availed himself of the first opportunity to seek the now infamous youth out. That opportunity came with the first hunting foray the Grand Marshal made—now reluctantly made—out of the castle since he had happened upon the young lover who had melted years off his felt age and made his penis a strong sword upon demand once more.

Cleus was gliding along the corridor in the Grand Marshal's apartments that afternoon when a strong hand reached out from behind a hanging tapestry and pulled the young man into the darkness behind. Raum devoured Cleus' lips with fervent kisses. Cleus, in turn, climbed Raum's pelvis with his thighs, and Raum fucked him deeply and long, pushing Cleus against the wall of the castle behind the shimmering tapestry and bouncing the shoulder blades of his prey mercilessly against the hard stone.

Thus were reunited the lovers—the son of King Cletar and the Nubian princess Nailah, but known only to King Severmist as his own catamite, and, Raum, who had been banished from Severmist's court for being found lying with Cleus to the almost certain death of spying inside the besieged High Castle of the Tharsisians as long as his wits could keep him alive.

Afterward the two slithered off to Raum's own humble room, and Raum gave Cleus a proper and prolonged fucking, Cleus on his back, legs akimbo and pelvis thrust up to received Raum's young, strong cocking, being ridden hard and for a great distance in contrast to the old Grand Marshal's almost pitiful pokings, and Raum stroking Cleus to multiple comings with thumb rubbing piss slit through the center of the golden cock ring.

"What are you doing here?" Raum asked through heavy breathing after they had spent themselves and were embracing, each part of them held as closely together as possible. "It would be the death of you if you were discovered. Did the Grand Marshal capture you without realizing who he had?"

"Nay, the Grand Marshal captured me because I meant him to—because the Watchman willed him to," Cleus answered. And then he laughed. He became immediately more serious, though. "We are getting nowhere with this siege, and the time of King Severmist's passing is close at hand. The Watchman declares it is time to put the kingdoms in the hands of the rightful heir, and I mean to aid that by delivering Tharsis into the hands of a new high king at long last."

"A heavy task," Raum whispered, his voice displaying his fear for his young lover. "You have seen how it is with the Tharsisians. How strong Tharsis is."

"But not as strong as it was before I came," Cleus said.

"What do you mean? What are you planning? What can I do to help?"

"Many questions, and I love you all the more, Raum, master of my seed, for your last question. What we must do is divide King Kleemus and the Grand Marshal. The strength of Tharsis has been their strong union. I have already started weakening that. And then I must be put within striking distance of the king at the right moment. There are, indeed, actions you can take to serve those ends."

"Command my hand, my liege," Raum said.

"Fuck my hole; mingle your seed with mine," Cleus countered, and then both young men laughed, as Raum proceeded to do just that.

* * * *

From that point began the campaign of Cleus and Raum to divide the Tharsisians' strength.

The king was already irritated at the Grand Marshal's unaccustomed absences, and while Cleus made sure that the Grand Marshal was abed fucking him as much of the time as possible, Raum was working on the king, asking him if he knew of the new, young, mesmerizing dancer the Grand Marshal had acquired. Asking the king if the Grand Marshal had ever offered to share the delights of watching Cleus perform.

The king had not been so invited. Indeed, before Raum started mentioning the possibility, he'd never thought of this being a slight at all. But the king was already just a bit unhappy with the Grand Marshal, and now he wanted to assert his kingship.

He commanded the Grand Marshal to bring the dancer Cleus before him in a private audience of just the three of them. And the Grand Marshal, seeing nothing amiss afoot, quickly brought the young Cleus, perfumed and fluffed up and sensuously costumed, forth to the king's private chambers.

Cleus danced a dance of passion and provocative display for the king, a dance that wound up with Cleus only in a golden belt, his gold snake bicep bracelets, his nipple and cock rings, and a warm smile on his face and a fluttering of his long eyelashes over obsidian-black eyes, his face turned toward the king, but his channel lowered into the lap of the overcome-with-lust Grand Marshal.

Three days later, at the king's strong suggestion, the Grand Marshal ventured out on another one of his hunting trips into the forests on the valley side of the High Castle. When he returned, however, he found the gates of the castle closed to him and a large force of the Akamantis coming over the hill. Needless to say the next gates the Grand Marshal entered weren't those of the High Castle.

The king was not seen out of his apartments for two weeks after that, busy as he was in discovering the charms of his new lover, the dancer Cleus.

Toward the end of that period, the king found Cleus lying on his couch, naked and despondent, one afternoon. The king dropped his own robes, came in beside Cleus, lifted his young lover's leg, and thrust a cock that hadn't been this hard for anyone else in years into the young god's passage. Although Cleus returned his kisses and murmured his love and devotion and praised the masterful cocking of the king, the king sensed a continued despondency.

"What is wrong, my fine young lover? I sense you are sad."

"It is only thinking of the future, sire. I want nothing more than for this to go on forever—your magnificent strong cock showing me new avenues to paradise daily. But where is it going? What is to become of us? The barbarians are at the gate. I fear for our lives. I could not bear our lives to change from what we have become."

"Never fear, my love," the king said. "I have a secret."

"A secret?" Cleus asked, his eyes full of innocence. He turned his face to the king's and nibbled on his ear, while his hand went to the king's rouged nipples.

"Yes, a secret. A secret passageway. We can escape into the mountains whenever we need to. And I have another, hidden castle in the mountains, not far from here, and stronger than this one. We are safe. We will always be safe."

"A secret passageway." Cleus repeated.

"Yes, I will show it to you. A passageway to a water gate coming out in a cave by a mountain stream."

And after Cleus had fucked the king to heaven once more, the king, indeed, showed Cleus the passageway to safety. And Cleus showed Raum the passageway that could be used in either direction. Then Raum, on a clear night within the week, when he was standing duty on the castle walls at the sea side, shot off the fire arrow with message attached that was a prearranged one-way communications means between the forces of King Severmist and their spy within the High Castle.

And on the night that the army of King Severmist crept into the cave beside the mountain stream and under the castle walls and into the very center of the castle keep, Cleus was abed with the king of the Tharsisians.

Cleus was on his back with King Kleemus knelt between his legs, sheathing his sword inside Cleus' channel. And at the first hint of the sounds Cleus was waiting to hear, he unsheathed his own dirk knife from under one of the pillows and sheathed it again up through the underbelly of the king of the Tharsisians.

"Thus it is for traitors, a traitor to his own cousin," Cleus murmured lovingly in Kleemus' ear as Kleemus grunted his last breaths. "And this is for my father, King Cletar," Cleus continued, his voice raised in triumph, as he pulled the knife out and plunged it in yet again.

He was standing, in robes of gold, beside the bed of the dead king, taking on a kingly stance as the forces of the Aram and Akamantis—his forces—rushed in the room to celebrate Prince Cleus' victory over the Tharsisians, undeniably won by wit and cleverness where brute force could not prevail.

Chapter Five: Prophecy Fulfilled

"You are pensive and sad of countenance, Cleus, when I would think you would be leaping with joy—on top of the world."

"Perhaps it is just the shock of your dispatching King Severmist at nearly the same instant that I was the undoing of King Kleemus. You surprise me, Watchman. I have observed you often working through other men, but hardly ever by your own hand."

"Oh, the Lords of Soso and Jerzu were ever so helpful," the Watchman responded. "They have ever borne a grudge against Severmist for using—and then losing—Toma. I do believe each one of them was deeply in love with his talented channel. And then, when Severmist moved against his own cousin, the two lords believed one or both of them would be next."

"And the lords? Where are they now?"

"Dispatched as well. It was rather messy, I'm afraid. They did not die well."

None of this helped with the pensiveness in the dusky young prince that the Watchman had discerned.

He had waited to approach Cleus in the king's chamber of the Enua palace until Raum had finished with him and had left the chamber.

The lovemaking between the two had moved the Watchman and made him mourn what he knew and accepted was the ending of any relationship he himself might have with Toma. Cleus was stretched, half on his side, half on his belly on the king's bier in the center of the chamber and Raum was kneeling over him, hands kneading the dusky beauty's shoulders, and cock buried deep in Cleus' channel. Cleus was moaning his pleasure and acceptance and moving his hips in rhythm with the pumping of Raum's well-trained staff. The taking was languid, as if they had forever. As if that was a choice Cleus could make. As the taking continued, they both become more vocal in their moans, and Raum lowered his body on Cleus', stretching out along the line of his body and moving him onto his belly. Raum was encasing him from above, touching him at every point he possibly could with his own body. His arms were stretched along Cleus', and the Watchman would have thought they had drifted off into sleep, were motionless, except for the entwining movement of their fingers merged together, the wave-like motion of Raum's hips and Cleus' pelvis, and the curling and uncurling of Cleus' long, sensuous toes to the rhythm of the fuck.

At length both gave a low cry and the intensity of the movement at their loins quickened—but only momentarily, as they both gave out a long, low sigh and relaxed their bodies in one entwined whole. They slept then, but only briefly. Raum knew his position. His life, his function at court, had not changed. To Cleus' low, huskily voiced objections, Raum raised himself from the platform and padded out of the chamber. Now was not the time for the court to have to officially acknowledge Raum's function in Cleus' life.

"I saw you with Raum, just now," the Watchman said when Cleus had dozed briefly and returned groggily to life. "Is that what has made you sad?"

"You see everything," Cleus said. And then he gave a quiet laugh, but it was not a happy laugh.

"I have seen you raised from the womb to manhood," the Watchman said. "Our family was small, there all those years on the beach at Gela. It would have been hard to miss what developed between you and Raum. Is that what is troubling you?"

"Yes," Cleus answered in almost inaudible tones and after a long pause.

"You are thinking on Cletar, your royal family, and how all of this complexity and treachery began, are you not? How he was. That he would not lay with a woman, would not take up his responsibility to the succession of the high kingship."

"Yes."

"And you do not want to do to the nation what your father did."

"No."

"Raum means so much to you that you give this relationship such high regard?"

130

"Yes. But I am prepared. As is Raum. If I am to be high king, I will take the responsibility fully. I will be a Cresum, not a Cletar."

"But you would rather just be the commander of the kingdoms forces, would you not, and partner solely with Raum?"

"You know everything. Yes, yes, of course I would."

"The oracle knew it would be so. The oracle knew and had faith in the future that I did not. And I believe it is the oracle, the Oracle at Noto, working for the gods, that has given you that trait of Cletar. It is nothing to be ashamed of, my son. You have done all that could be asked of you. What you have with Raum is something beautiful; not something you need—or should have to—deny."

Cleus stood there, naked, both in body and soul, before his mentor and protector, the Watchman. There was nothing he could say. In days of joy, he was consumed by sadness and the heavy burden that he saw as his.

"Look up, Cleus," the Watchman said in a commanding, yet gentle tone. "What do you see?"

Cleus looked up. What he saw surprised and perplexed him. But he could not discern what the Watchman was trying to tell him, what was happening here.

"Hello, brother," a voice emerged from the shadows. The sound was followed by the appearance of a small, but well-formed Nubian.

"Toma. Is it you? Have you abandoned your life and family in Favara to return to us at court to take up duties here? If so, you are happily welcome. I seem to be bereft of advisers, the principle ones having recently been dispatched for treachery."

"No, I've brought my wife and son with me," Toma answered simply. "The Watchman called and I answered."

"The Watchman called you to court?" Cleus asked, still confused.

"The misunderstanding is mine," the Watchman interjected. "The oracle and the gods knew what they were doing. But it was a mistake I'm glad I made—and I believe the gods would not have permitted it if it were not a good thing for the kingdoms."

"A mistake?" Cleus was still very much in the dark.

131

"You are not to be high king, Cleus," the Watchman said. "The Oracle never meant that you were to be. Your making was by my making—because I misunderstood; I did not have enough faith in the oracle. But you can be the key support to the high king—and you can still have what you desire. You can still command the forces of the kingdoms and partner exclusively with Raum."

"Not the high king?"

"No. Does that trouble you much? I would be very wrong if I thought that it did."

"No, no, it doesn't trouble me, Watchman. It would lift a heavy burden from me. I would be overjoyed. But how . . . who . . . ?"

"I'm surprised I didn't see it. If he had been like other men of Aram in appearance, I'm sure I would have. The oracle's prophecy was that the direct line of King Cresum would lead to the high king who would unify the kingdoms of the region. My mistake was in not realizing that this man already existed before I schemed to coax a male heir from the loins of King Cletar. My further mistake was not seeing that unity is in the ruling, the governing, not the military conquest. You can be a great soldier, a commander, but Toma has it in him to be a wise and fair ruler.

"The direct line from Cresum led through his oldest surviving son. The Nubian princes Nailah need not have lain with Cletar. She had already borne a son directly from Cresum. The moment Cletar was slain, Toma became that eldest surviving son. Toma is the gods-anointed high king of the lands of Aram, Akamantis, Tharsis, and the Kerastis. And he can and has begotten sons."

Toma flinched and turned to the Watchman.

"Yes, Toma. Your Maia is bearing another son. What I can and do declare here and now is that the Prophecy of Noto has been fulfilled. King Toma is the high king. Long may his lineage reign in peace and strength—protected by the military prowess and fealty of his brother, Cleus."

The King's Men

Chapter One: Peril on Sea and Land

It has never ceased to amaze me that they never see us and yet we know all. The nobility live their lives with their every whim and need taken care of. And yet if someone asked them how that happened, they invariably would stop and ponder and still not know. Those of us who do all of that for them are invisible. There is no limit to what they will do or say in front of us and believe that they were alone, that no one else was there to see—and, more interestingly—to see through them.

Thus it was with those at the court of my king, Claude de Lusane, the man my lady, the Princess—now Queen—Blanche, brought me to and might have loved—perhaps as much as I came to love him. Although of that I must not speak. The high born can think on it and indulge in it. But not one such as me. Unless, of course, I am wanted in that way. But ugly and deformed as I am, I almost never have been wanted that way—at least not since I was young—even though many around me have been. A pity that. Although I have been fucked. Yes, I have. I have exchanged my loyalty for the cock as well as any noble has. Perhaps not as often. Certainly not often enough.

Thus it was that after that harrowing, storm-tossed month at sea and the indignity of the Limonean prison—they called it a castle, but if it was, I'd hate to see how their serfs live—I came to be witness to all that happened in that momentous first half year at the Kibrit court. Perhaps not all, but enough of it to make clear the what and why of it, holding puzzle pieces that none of the confused or scheming lead actors in the drama had in their possession—or bothered to look for, even though they nestled right under their eyes. And all just by being there, standing in the room, being invisible to those who were playing high stakes with their lives—and with the lives of others.

And perhaps that's another significant difference between one such as me and the nobility. I have nothing to lose or to gain—it's all on sufferance from them. They, on the other hand, have so much at stake, and it is all on risk during their every waking moment.

* * * *

What appeared at the time the most fearful and endangering moments of my life paled in the light of the to-the-death intrigue I encountered in King Claude's supposedly sedate court. The sea voyage from Holland to the shores of the island of Kibrit ended, thanks to the capriciousness of the storms of nature, with my lady and her retinue landing, amid the wreckage of the only ship of the flotilla that survived, on an enemy shore rather than in the safe harbor of her newly wed husband. And this not to mention, as the queen warned me never to speak of it, what she had to do for us to survive to see the king's court.

The welcome Simon Limona gave to my lady, Blanche, at his castle in the harbor of his city state on the southern coast was both menacing and just within the bounds of propriety—or so I have been commanded to say of it. There is a code of conduct and deportment among the nobility of Europe now, one driven by the Holy See in this age that centers on the crusades to reestablish the faith in the Holy Land, but it was not understood here on Kibrit. There was no love lost at all between Simon Limona and King Claude. Limona was hanging onto his miniscule kingdom by a last death hold against the increasing might of the king. And the island of Kibrit we landed upon is at the corner of the civilized world. And as long as I have lived there, I've never been sure about which side of the "civilized" line it rested on.

Claude, already the king of Damascus and Acre, had been granted suzerainty over the Mediterranean island of Kibrit in recognition of his defending of the faith in two previous crusades—a prodigious effort for one so young, the king barely having reached the age of two score. His first crusade, in the company of his aged father, King Claxton, had been the old king's last. And Claude's next crusade had been under his own banner as king and had been the campaign in which he had subdued and subjugated Damascus and Acre.

The only problem with the pope's gift was that there already existed city state kingdoms on Kibrit. To establish his kingship there—and acquire what would be the first substantive base for his rule—Claude first had to subdue the island. This he had methodically been doing—he was a suburb military leader and warrior in his own right—right up to the very moment I first laid eyes on his physical visage.

I had seen paintings, for true, of him, exchanged with the House of Holland during the negotiations over his yet-to-be-consummated marriage to Blanche, and he had certainly been handsome and commanding in these. But the paintings were nothing in the stead of the magnificence of the golden-haired young king when I first set my eyes on the in-the-flesh man. I could not see how any man who might succumb to the charms of another man could resist him. And I soon could see—although many others apparently could not—that, with King Claude, many were the men who couldn't resist him.

King Claude would not have been in the harbor city of Paphaes on the island's west coast to receive Blanche even if her flotilla had not been thrown off course by the sudden storm on the Mediterranean. The marriage to Blanche was important, yes, but it was secondary to the need for there to be a welcoming and safe home for Blanche to come to and for the young king to start his married life with a queen—with a queen who could bear him sons to solidify the rule of the house of Lusane. So, instead

135

of awaiting her arrival at Paphaes, he was in the north, on the ridge of the chain of mountains running east and west the length of Kibrit, attacking the last mountaintop bastion castle, save one, of the last holdout Kibrit independent kingdom, save Simon Limona's small city state. At the moment I first saw the king, the castle of St. Jerome had fallen into his hands, and he had broken the back of the proud and ancient kingdom of Turionia, which had been forged on the eastern and northern coast of Kibrit by the remnants of the victory fleet returning home from the Trojan war that had been separated from the main flotilla and washed up on the shores of a paradise even more enticing to them than their Acadian meadows.

Perhaps in fairness to the king, I should write something in response to the subsequent rumors that have been floated about the cool relationship between King Claude and Queen Blanche in that first year of their marriage—one arranged a continent away with, by custom, neither husband nor wife ever seeing each other in the flesh until many months after the marriage. It is true that Blanche did not conceive a son in that first year—and, although not fully relevant—the rumors of the king's preference are also true. But it's not true that Blanche hated the king from the outset because he let her fall into the hands of the enemy and placed his conquest of Turionia above her honor and comfort. And it is not true that she denied him for that year as a result—or that she believed him of a different persuasion from the outset.

Of the rumor that Simon Limona enjoyed the king's marriage bed and the queen's secret purse ever before Claude did that surfaced later in their married life when Blanche brazenly took on lovers and the king nearly as brazenly danced on the cock of his lieutenant—and that, I am proud to say, largely through my own intrigue—I will surely here try to resist attesting to.

First, Blanche was foisted upon Claude in a lie. Few, of course, know that, and history certainly will know nothing of it. Only such as I who silently stand in the presence of scheming, unseen and unregarded, within the court, learn of such things. Blanche was not the young fourth daughter of the House of Holland, as claimed. She was the older, second daughter. None

136

of the daughters paraded in public, so none but the inner court in Vollendam knew anything of the truth. Thus Blanche, as beautiful as she was, was at the very edge of child bearing.

And it was not true that she showed any coolness toward Claude at all. She melted at the sight of Claude and she lifted her skirts and opened her legs to him whenever she could get him to lie with her. As a salamander on the wall at the court at Vollendam, I can attest to the truth that Blanche easily lifted her skirts to any man as handsome as Claude—or certainly any big-cocked man. Later, of course, the reality of their relationship changed. But even then, she lusted for him and would have overlooked all and lain with him if ever he looked at her.

But eventually Claude, who in the first few months of their meeting, fucked—excuse my baldness, but, as I am no gentleman of the nobility but am a man of the earth, this is going to be a tale of honest baldness—his new wife as often as he could in his desire for an heir, came to realize his inclinations were otherwise. And on the subject of bald language for the acts of man, let me say that it is my firm conviction that if the nobles can do what they do so freely and openly, I can certainly call what they do what it is. There came a time when I believed that the nobles lived for the fuck and for the fuck alone—either fucking another in body or in soul and for gain and the command of all. Or for mere survival. And I'm not so sure I think otherwise even now.

I see no need to hold back in the description and revelation here. I write here for my own pleasure, and parchment can easily be assigned to the fire as surely as this will be ere I finish writing it. I am all aglow, fresh from a most satisfying fuck, which comes so infrequently at my age and withering condition. The monks sent me back to my rooms for fear of my health, saying I looked flushed. And of course I am flushed. I have danced on a cock with their stable boy, a comely half-blind, well-hung lad who claims that my old channel is as tight and supple as he would want, but, truth be known, is, as I said, half blind and at the age and temperament where he would fuck a sheep, pig, or dog given the opportunity. My heart is pounding and my mind is soaring. And if it be my desire to prolong the ecstasy by dallying here and writing down the true, unabridged history of Claude's house of Lusane, where is the harm in that? No one but me will be seeing it.

But, returning to the thread of my revelations, there was none of this upon-sight rejection and coolness by Blanche for the rumor of Claude's deviations. And there were no such deviations in Claude's preferences—despite the overflowing of it in the minds of many of the king's men swirling about him at the time—in those first few months.

And, if secrets of secrets must be revealed—and I hesitate in writing of this and only do so because I know it is no one but myself that will read it, perhaps not putting it to the fire but perhaps putting it aside to revel in in post-fuck reverie the next time I find the stable boy alone and fondling his precious staff—it will not be by me. The nobles of the Lusanes can have no idea that I know any of this—let alone that the monks have now taught me, in my seclusion—to write and read. But of deep secrets, I must say, meaning no harm to the House of Lusane— that when Blanche did produce her son, it was not a true son of Claude—or Blanche for that matter—but a result of her own scheming with a willing noble family whose daughter had been compromised so that Blanche was not to be cast away from the husband she adored no matter what his change in interests. If nothing else, Blanche wanted to be queen. And as queen, she could command cocks to rise to her desires.

However I digress—and perhaps to sustain interest, I will not dwell—at least yet—on the trials of Blanche and the survivors of her retinue in the castle tower of Limonea, with her sneering host, Simon, making all assortments of threats and suggestions against her honor and life—ones, as written for the history, never carried beyond voicing but ones for which Simon paid with his kingdom and his life within the fortnight, in any event.

I will, instead, pick up my pen next to regain the narrative from the moment, as an unnoticed salamander on the wall, I shared in Claude's victory at the castle of St. Jerome and the spinning out of the tale of triumph, scheming, treachery, and glory of the King's Men.

Chapter Two: To the Victor

It was a day that changed history when I finally was passed through the lines and stood before the chamberlain of King Claude in the castle keep of St. Jerome's. The battle had just been won, the castle within a half hour of final capitulation. Soldiers, sweating and running in blood themselves, were still walking among the vanquished laying about where they had dropped, checking for life, and extinguishing it when they found it.

The three of them—the three principle men I was to follow with my eyes and ears and interest for the next half year and more, with them rarely even knowing I was in attendance— were standing there in the flush of victory, leaning on their blood-stained broadswords. They were still heaving and panting under their heavy chain-mail trappings, and congratulating themselves and each other on the penultimate island kingdom gained in their campaign to take all and to bring peace at last to this fecund island. There yet was Cantria castle further east, nearly to the end of the mountain chain and within smoke-signal sighting of the Musselmen coast of Turkey. But the fall of that was a foregone conclusion, and King Claude even now was telling his men, Guy, Duke of Gano, and the other, younger, fairer king's man, Sir Rene deRogair, that they mayhaps would just lay siege to Cantria and starve it out rather than waste more man flesh on seizing it. Sir Rene, always the more compassionate and less bloodthirsty of Claude's key lieutenants, had just been reporting on the horrendous cost of life to Claude's forces that had been the winning of St. Jerome's.

I liked Sir Rene the instant I saw him—and I never have faltered in liking him and respecting him. Nor have I faltered in having sympathy for what I could see at a glance when I was ushered into the periphery of their presence at St. Jerome was his worshipful stance toward his king. And I'm not talking in a religious sense.

I saw the same lustful, wanting desire in the eyes of the dark, bulkier, more menacing Guy for his king and I immediately feared for the golden-haired and serious-demeanored monarch, even loving him then, at first sight in the flesh, as much as his two lieutenants obviously did.

As much as I instantly liked and respected Rene, I did the opposite for Guy. And that initial assessment never changed in my view either. I knew immediately that all of the grief in Claude's life would be a result of Guy's life, and I pledged from that moment—transferring my fealty and service at that moment from Blanche to Claude no matter what livery I wore—never to let Guy alone in Claude's presence if I could help it. Alas, in that I failed.

"What ho?" Claude asked when the chamberlain approached him in regards to my presence. "Who is this and what news does he have of my queen, Blanche? I see he is in the livery of the Vollendam court, although the ride here must have been a difficult one, for his livery is in tatters. She has landed safely in Paphaes, I trust."

The chamberlain murmured to him, and I saw the concern, rising to anger, in Claude's voice. And then he instantly became the king decision maker that had always been his talent.

"I will leave the consolidation of St. Jerome to you, Guy. I must off to Lefkosea"—which I knew to be the king's principle city on the plain between the coasts and the two mountain regions of the island—"to receive Simon's delegation and his demands for Blanche's safe release."

Then he turned to Sir Rene and said, "No matter what happens diplomatically with Simon, upon Blanche's safe return, I want Limonea—and Simon—crushed. You will pick out the best men able to travel, Rene, and move south, ready to pounce upon Limonea at my signal."

Important diplomatic and military dispositions having been made, I was awed and pleased that he had a word for me. He turned to the chamberlain and said, "Blanche's man must be tired from the journey Simon set him on. He looks not even recovered from the shipwreck as yet. See that he is rested here and given clothes marking him of my inner chambers, and then, when he is able, send him on to Lefkosea. You will, I am sure, want to speak with him on the likes and comforts of his mistress, my queen."

The chamberlain after a few terse words for me, told me to follow in Guy's train for now—that Guy's chamber servants were presently in even worse shape than I was and that I could be of use in the next few hours—that he would find some place for me to feed and to rest when Guy no longer needed me.

It was thus that I quickly and fully came to understand the cruel nature and animal capacities of the Duke of Gano. I trust that I learned in a single evening what his close comrade and king hadn't learned earlier and never really would, despite having grown up where the man was a chief counselor of the man who was king before Claude.

When the king, Sir Rene, and the chamberlain had all departed, there remained Duke Guy, who walked, with me and several others in his train, into the great hall of the castle. There, in the hay at the corners of the room, in the long shadows cast by the torches set high on the chamber's stone walls, the privileged of the soldiers of Lefkosea were making sport, amid great laughter and loud wailing, with the women of the castle who had not been able to steal away. Young and old alike, the women were beset by groups of men, some holding their bared legs wide, others making them to suck, and the most privileged of the soldiers taking first duty between their legs.

This was barbarity that I had never seen nor imagined in the civilized cities of northern Europe. I supposed that this was normal crusade fare, but even with that, I doubted that either King Claude or Sir Rene would have countenanced this debauchery if they had remained on the field.

Some younger men and boys were similarly beset, but most of the captives who remained alive—young and older men, very few left of warrior age—were huddled together in a quivering, heads-down mass in the center of the hall.

Immediately upon entering the hall, and as those in train filtered in, Duke Guy strode to the great table at the far end of the hall and bounded up on it, obviously knowing precisely what he was about at that moment.

Ignoring the raping in full flux at the edges of the hall, he unbuckled his breeches and lowered them to where he could bring forth a monster bludgeon of a half-hard cock. Holding this erect in his hand, he boomed forth in a commanding voice.

"Any of you captive men who pledges willingness to entertain this tonight will not be killed by my hands. The rest can start saying their prayers now. Let me see the hands."

Only two hands went up—that of a young man, barely more than a boy, and another of a fairly formed man of some more years who was dressed for service in the master's chambers rather than for war.

"Ah, disappointing," Guy growled. "I lust for more than two after a battle such as this. But nothing to do about that."

He turned to the man who appeared to be his closest attendant, a young, chain-mail-clad man of steamy eyes who moved lithely and assuredly through the chamber as of having a special status with the duke. The young man spoke first, showing a privilege that I instantly discerned and marked. I would not make an enemy of this man if I could help it. "How do you wish these two prepared, sire, and what of the rest?"

"The young one horsed, I believe. And the other one on the suspending rod, I think. Find the master bedchamber and set the apparatuses up near that. And have this man," he continued, gesturing at me—indicating for the first time that he even knew I was there, which came as both a jolt and a warning to me—I was to learn that he saw and knew far more than one would surmise—"have this man clean the bedchamber before I arrive. I have the captain of the guards to sort out first. But be quick about it. And be prepared to attend yourself. I feel the victory, and with only two volunteers, I will want to share it with you later."

"Yes, my lord," the younger man said, and I noticed a twitch in his sensually thick lips and a gleam in his eye. "And what of the rest of these captives here?"

"Cleanse the castle of them," Guy said, his eyes looking hard. "We want only loyal Lefkoseans in residence here on the morrow."

I got to the master bedchamber a bit before Guy arrived, so I had time to control the shock and cover my demeanor as I moved around, tidying up from what probably was the previous master's last stand in his inner sanctum. Guy's lieutenant, Guido, who I later had much reason to know intimately and who I learned to be an Italian of a noble but impoverished Venetian family, had already seen to the removal of any corpses and the mopping up of most of the blood. I did have to change the bedding, though, as it was evident that this was where the previous occupant had met his demise.

Before I had reached the chamber, located in a tower ascended to by a stone spiral staircase, I had to proceed through a chamber two flights below the bedchamber—and then again, a chamber that had a single, raised bed in it, with a straw mattress and a rough-textured blanket covering it. The lower chamber is where the two captives had been taken. The youth, already moaning and babbling, was bent on his belly over a saddle stand that must have been brought from the stables, and his wrists and ankles were bound at the base of the four legs. He was naked, his skin a translucent white and silky soft as a baby's.

Across the chamber, a scaffold had been erected, and the older man, also naked, was suspended from that with his wrists tied at the crossbar. In contrast to the youth, he wasn't making a sound. His eyes were roaming the room, taking it all in, calculating.

Guido had managed—miraculously in terms of the time that had been available—to clean his body of the blood of war and now wore a soft, silken, blue tunic, which was open on his chest down almost to his navel and which revealed a well-worked and darkened by the sun body and a profusion of soft, curly hair.

I couldn't help going hard at the sight of him, and I instantly knew that he had this power over Guy as well.

I busied myself in the bedchamber until the sounds drew me down two flights of stairs, where I stood in the shadows and watched Guy at work.

He was naked now. His body was riddled with scars, but it was magnificent in its hardness and bulk. He was in huge erection, his balls heavy and also hairy, as was the rest of his body—dark haired even in his somewhat advanced age. His chest and belly muscles were as if he'd never taken his armor off.

He was breathing heavily, taxed but joyous by the efforts of flicking the hand whip he held in one hand on the exposed and silky-skinned buttocks and thighs of the youth, who was screaming and writhing under the lash as best he could. Four fingers of Guy's other hand were buried between the folds of the youth's butt cheeks and ere he was finished, I am sure I saw the whole fist go in, to the sound of much distress from the young man.

The man suspended across the room was looking on almost with disinterest, his eyes still scrutinizing the scene closely, calculating. Guido was standing by one of the stone columns holding the ceiling up, his eyes hooded, licking his lips.

The youth cried out in evidence of virginity while Guy was working his cock between his butt cheeks in substitute of the fingers and fist. There was no change in the responses of the suspended man, but I saw Guido's hand going to the hem of his own tunic and raising that to reveal a nice, plump, hard cock, which he proceeded to work as Guy brutally fucked the youth.

In all honestly, and knowing I am determined to tell the story fully and completely, I must acknowledge that my hand went to relieve my member as well. But my eyes were on Guido, not on Guy.

After the duke finished, Guido handed him a tunic and, with my attendance—Guy, I'm sure, in his exaltation not even realizing an extra pair of hands was present—it was pulled over his head and he went to supper.

An hour later, the activity below drew me from the bedchamber again and I stole the two flights down the stairs.

The scene was entirely different with the man suspended from the scaffold. The youth was still there, bent over the saddle frame, but he was unconscious—or dead. I knew not which at the time. And, in the end, it didn't matter much.

Guy was already fucking the man suspended in the frame, from the front, his pelvis plastered to the man's uprolled hips. But, although Guy was in ecstasy, he wasn't in control as he had been with the youth. The suspended man had his legs wrapped around Guy's thick waist and he was the one doing the fucking, Guy was just standing there in a half crouch, entranced and trembling, as the suspended man pumped the ducal cock with his channel. He had also lured Guy's lips to his and they were kissing deeply. Guy's hands were locked at the back of the man's head, keeping them close together, seeming to want to merge his body with the captives.

When Guy ejaculated, it was he who lost his balance and fell back onto his buttocks on the chamber floor.

Looking up in wonder, he groaned the question. "You have done this before, haven't you?"

"It was what I did here in the castle," the man answered softly. "I can do so much more unbound. I can fuck you as you have never been fucked before."

Standing, with both Guido and me moving to him, Guy muttered. "This one. In my bed tonight."

"Is that wise?" Guido asked. And, although I don't think Guy heard it or understood it, I could hear the hurt and concern in Guido's voice.

"I see to the night guard now. I want him in my bed when I return. Have him washed first."

"And what of the youth?"

"I have taken him to heaven. Now send him there. It will not be by my hand, though, as I pledged."

When we were alone—at least I felt it was just Guido and me, with me feeling the depth of his grief and anger—Guido commanded me to go to the chamber above and await further command. Two soldiers were untying the youth from the saddle frame. I think I heard a moan, so he must have still been alive, although that knowledge gave me no comfort. Two other soldiers were releasing the man from the scaffold frame and leading him up the stairs, with Guido following them.

I went up the stairs, as bidden to do, and sat on the straw mattress of the cot.

The two soldiers came down the stairs and then continued below.

A few moments later, I heard the sound of a struggle from above and I stood and pressed my fist to my mouth. Somehow I knew this was a time when I must be invisible to actions unfolding right before me. I knew in my heart and head what was transpiring—and why.

Thus I was not surprised—but still shocked—when I saw the captive scrambling down the stairs into the chamber I occupied. Close behind him, though, came Guido. He had a knife in his hand. There was scant struggle before the captive pitched down the bottom half of the stone stairs on his face.

145

Guido called out and the two soldiers reemerged from the chamber below—where they had been waiting within the hearing distance of a command, for whatever reason they were there.

In seconds, the lifeless body of the captive was gone and only the smear of blood on the stairs remained as evidence that anything at all had happened here.

Guido met Guy in the chamber below. There was silence, followed by Guy's raised voice in anger, which was quickly stifled into calmer discussion as the two moved up the stairs on which I was pulled back to the wall, trying my best to disappear into the shadows of a circular stone chamber with nothing in it but a cot and me.

Guido was telling Guy of the captive's attempt to escape and that he had fallen down the steps and broken his neck in his attempt to elude Guido's restraint in the chamber above. The duke was finding the explanation persuasive.

Guy didn't see me. I should not have been surprised. As he started up the stairs to the chamber above, also conveniently not seeing the smear of blood on the stone stair treads, Guido motioned to me and I followed.

I stood in the shadows of the bedchamber as Guido pulled the soft, blue tunic off his beautiful body and lay down in the center of the master's bed, arranging a bolster pillow under the small of his back and spreading his legs.

Guy stood there, at the foot of the bed, looking with lust upon his young lieutenant. I stepped forward at Guido's gesture and raised Guy's tunic over his head and stepped back, not, I'm sure, having taken Guy's notice at all.

I heard the almost animalistic sound coming from deep in Guy's throat, and he was upon Guido in a flash, thrusting hard and deeply inside Guido's channel, as Guido arched his back and turned his head and bit into the thick brocade material of the bed cloth. Despite what I was sure was a painful entry, I saw Guido immediately start to move his hips, drawing Guy deeper inside him and making his channel make love to Guy's cock—making Guy forget the entertainment that he had anticipated enjoying at this point and that had been snatched from him.

146

After Guy had ejaculated from the second taking, he rolled off Guido and went off into a satisfied, snoring sleep. Guido rose from the bed and came to me. "Attend me below," he whispered, as he moved toward the stand with the water jar on it.

I went down one flight and sat on the cot. When Guido came down, he was still naked, carrying the blue tunic at his side.

"Turn and bend over the bed and let down your breeches," he said in a low, hoarse voice.

"But, sir," I involuntarily—and foolishly—muttered in surprise.

"Do not question. Do not ever question. Do it."

I turned, unbound my belt, and my breeches fell to the floor.

I gave a muffled cry—as much in ecstasy and want as in surprise and shock—as, holding my hips with his hands, Guido entered me and began to take me in long, strong strokes.

He bent his mouth to my ear. "You want it, don't you? I could see it in your eyes. And it's from me that you want it."

In surprise, I answered, "Yes." I was not invisible to all nobles, I was learning. It was a good lesson. It made me more wary in a court infused with intrigue and treachery such as the Court of Holland never experienced in my knowledge.

"Well, listen and listen good. There is more of this. I doubt you get much. But whether or not I ever fuck you again, remember this. I am the duke's man. Body and soul. But though you serve the queen and the king and the duke, you are *my* man. It is my back—and my cock, if you want more of it—that you watch out for. Do you understand?"

"Yes," I moaned. And I kept right on moaning, not wanting him to stop.

Chapter Three: Victory Celebration

I try not to speak ill of anyone, especially of my own countrymen, but the world would have been much better if Queen Blanche's understeward, Kobus, had gone down in one

147

of the other ships in the storm. He was only with us because his parents were close friends of Blanche's father and they had a son who embarrassed them with his brazenness and the mischief he got in and who they wanted to see doing well—but doing it a world away from them.

I do believe that Kobus created mischief just for mischief's sake. And I don't believe he wanted the duke any more than he had wanted Sir Rene before him. But the moment Guido and Kobus laid eyes on each other, they were mortal enemies. And Guy was the object that they both unconsciously selected as the trophy. When the time came for Blanche to want a spy in Guy's bed, Kobus was all for the challenge.

I did not object to Kobus' very being because of this. In my mind, the duke wasn't worth fighting over and either one of the lads were welcome to him. But not all that Kobus did went for harm; it was Kobus who subsequently, as I will, in time, set down in ink here, awakened Rene to what one man could do to another. And after Kobus had left him and Rene realized that his true focus of desire was the king himself, this, perhaps, was the one catalyst that offset Guy's own desires to control the king and that set the kingdom in balance. For as the king, although he was a sexual dunce and self-denier enough not apparently to realize it until almost too late, had sensual feelings for both the dark, aggressive duke and the fair, in both aspect and attitude, Rene, the king had capacities to fall under the sway of Guy's darkness or Rene's gentle passion. Until Duke Guy saw Rene as competition for a long campaign to entrap and fuck—yes, fuck—fuck and control the king, however, the duke's schemes did not become murderous within the court of Lefkosea.

All appeared right with the world when I had been given passage from the castle St. Jerome and chamber service to Duke Guy and deeper service to his lieutenant, Guido, whose attentions I gloried in. If Guido had asked me to do anything for him in those three weeks I spent in the castle mountaintop as the duke oversaw the siege of the stronghold at Cantria and consolidation of the repopulation of the northern Kibrit coast with Lefkosea loyalists, I very well would have done it. I certainly forgot for his sake what I had seen in his flash of jealousy and clutching at the duke's favor. I had seen murder against the duke's express wishes, and I had not told the duke of it. If I myself were discovered in that, my life would have been forfeited.

When I arrived at the court in Lefkosea, though, my time and energy were immediately taken up in preparing for the arrival of Blanche and her retinue. The king had paid an emperor's ransom for her release and issued the apology for her intrusion on the shores of Limonea that Simon had demanded—along with giving written and attested assurance that Claude would recognize and mark the kingship of Simon over Limonea for all eternity.

As soon as Blanche and her people were safely on the road to Limonea, however, and well beyond any reach of Simon, the forces of Rene deRogair descended on the open gates of Limonea city. Rene did not permit rape and pillage, but the slaughter was near total.

Simon himself was spared, however. Rene brought him back, in chains, in an open ox cart to Lefkosea, where he was hung from the window of the highest tower of Claude's city castle for all to see. His crown was nailed to his head as he was lowered, crying for mercy on unhearing ears, out of the window. And his skeleton was still hanging there, marking, as Claude promised, that he reigned as the King of Limonea, one hundred and twenty years later when the Ottoman Turks overran and subjugated the island to another hundred years of their rule.

Blanche reached Lefkosea two weeks before Rene completed his subjugation of the Limoneans, and she was well established in the queen's chambers before his return.

I attended her in her chambers. I know that the king visited her and that she lifted her night skirts and opened her thighs to him willingly and that he pumped her cunt with youth and vigor. I heard cry of his release of seed inside her—again and again. He was a young and virile man. She was a beautiful woman who, as I well knew, was not unknown to a man's cock before the king's member visited her and who had the guile to make him enjoy his lying with her. She had wiles and potions and determination. She was no less determined to bear him a son before the heat of the coming summer than he was in doing his duty in producing a son.

The fact that he did not linger with her, did not play with her, or find any position of fucking her other than the one, unimaginative, belly to belly one was, I am sure, more a result of the little experience he had with such things. I had certainly seen Blanche being more inventive. If it was more than that—if it was an unrealized knowledge deep inside him that he wanted more, something different, or that someone else aroused him and moved him more than any woman could, I am quite sure he did not recognize it at the time.

It was such with the nobility. They didn't think deeply on these matters. They did not examine themselves or observe or question why and how every shallow whim was fulfilled for them by others without any of their own planning or effort, and this became enough in their lives—giving them lives of shallow surface whims.

I, of course, could see immediately that no matter how often the king appeared in Blanche's chambers and she lifted her skirts to him and spread her legs for him, that it was all shallow in performance even if deeper in the intent of them both.

But I'm being unfair, Blanche could see it as well. She was of the nobility. But she was also a world-wise woman. She knew when a man was just dallying with her, wanting to get his cock inside her just to be able to say he'd fucked one—or, in some cases all four—of the princesses of the House of Holland. And she knew when, like with her father, something more serious and moving was transpiring. Blanche and her elder sister were from one queen and the two younger princesses from another queen. Blanche's father's match with his first queen was one that developed into a deep love; the second one didn't go farther than the good of the state. The first queen died in childbirth—producing the king's fifth son. The Dutch king pined for years—even after he had taken a second wife. And then Blanche grew into the perfect likeness of her mother.

Blanche understood what that meant to her father and how her mere presence in the palace affected him. So, she had arranged the tryst that put him over the edge of propriety, even in the hedonist court at Vollendam, and fucked him willingly and lovingly and often—being her mother for him. And their parting when she boarded ship for the Mediterranean, already another king's wife, was a bittersweet farewell for both of them.

I, of course, was there for it all—in the chamber when she laid down under a succession of men, including her father—and more than one woman as well. I was there, in attendance to any shallow whim she might express while a cock or tongue was churning inside her—unseen, unregarded. Just a piece of the furniture.

The one thing that Blanche's lying under her father had taught her was that this new, young, virile king was not in love with her, or, she had to admit, in lust with her body either. Perhaps in time, though.

So, while determined to do her queenly duty, and with regret that the king's beautiful body was not matched with the ardor she had come to expect in a man, within weeks of her establishment at the Lefkosea court, Blanche was on the hunt.

And, as coincidence, when the dashing Sir Rene deRogair returned from Limonea in victory at the head of a small force that had assured the consolidation of the House of Lusane on the island of Kibrit, the pride and joy overflowed from him, making him even more stately and handsome than ever before.

I watched my queen, Blanche's, eyes go to Rene and assess him, at first, as worthy of riding, but then, upon seeing him look at his king, I saw her assessment change, seeing him more as a rival. Then I saw her eyes narrow and a slight little smile flit onto her face as she saw Simon, in rags, torn from once-regal attire that Blanche well remembered, cowed and quivering in his ox cart.

She had declared vengeance upon him, and now I saw that she would revel in what was to be done with him—knowing that he would take to the afterworld his knowledge of what he had done to her—or had thought he had done.

* * * *

It is perhaps time to delve into those brief weeks where the Queen of Kibrit, princess of the Holland Court, was the "guest" of Simon Limona.

Simon was a grizzled, wily old bird, having survived many an attempt to seize the small, but rich, piece of real estate he fancied to be—and somehow managed to sustain as—an independent city state. Tall and gaunt and sinewy, Simon had lived beyond his fiftieth year through guile and his readiness to work with his hands and his wit alongside his serfs in the terraced fields running up from his harbor town. His surroundings were niggardly, yet starkly beautiful, but he, himself, was a dandy when he was entertaining, dressing like a king and wanting all of his servants and serfs to see the vast difference between he and them. No wife having been able to survive him, he mostly lived sparingly and needed but little in the comforts of castle—as Blanche and her retinue quite quickly could attest to.

I truly believe he never intended to let Blanche or any of the rest of us live—that he planned to dally with us and then dispatch us, claiming no knowledge of a wreck upon his coast or a missing queen. Otherwise he would not have done what he did—and Blanche would not have had to do what she did.

The Limoneans, under Simon's direct supervision, were ruthless from the first moment Blanche's flagship was seen to be breaking up in the surf off the Limonea beach. As stragglers were struggling ashore, Simon was there, assessing each one as to position and usefulness. The Spanish sailors, as they reached the sand, gasping for breath, had their throats cut where they crouched. Even Blanche's priest confessor was run down as he waddled along the beach, habit bunched up around his waist, and quickly sent to heaven.

Blanche and her handmaidens and her close servants, which included me and her understeward, Kobus, were singled out, huddled together, and herded up to the ominous castle glowering over the city's harbor. There, in a cold, stone-clad chamber, we were left to shiver and husband and expand our fears for three nights.

On the fourth evening, Blanche and her servants were called out to supper with Simon. The handmaidens were left in the prison chamber to contemplate their fate.

A lavish banquet had been set out upon the table and seated at the head—in the only chair at the table—was Simon

Limona. He was dressed in regal splendor. His steel-gray hair had been trimmed to perfection and his goatee and mustache had been dressed with shining oil.

"Do not be shy, come forward my beautiful, Queen Blanche. I wish to honor you and your noble husband. I wish to feast."

"But there is no chair," Blanche responded haughtily. "A queen does not stand and sup as her lessers sit."

"Oh, I don't mean for you to stand, dear Blanche. Come. Oh, you are reluctant. Here, my men will help you."

Kobus and I watched, hoping this would be a time when we were invisible in the great hall although we soon felt hands of menace on our arms and backs too, as two men pulled Blanche forward to between the table and where Simon was sitting in his throne and pushed her down into the plates and serving dishes on the table, holding her down and in place with each holding a milky-white arm flat against the table top.

Leisurely, Simon pulled up her skirts one by one and when he got to her undergarments, he just ripped them away. He slapped her bare buttocks and laughed little appreciative laughs until her tender skin blushed. And then he stood, unlaced his cod piece, presented to her, and slowly pushed his way into . . . her ass channel.

At first, even though writhing under the insulting assault, Blanche said not a word. But at length, and to Simon's great surprise, she began to wiggle her hips more sensually and to moan of the power and size of him. She began to play on his vanity, speaking of the great pleasure he was giving her, declaring that, as a virgin, she had yet a greater gift to him, if he only but let her free to voluntarily give him the ultimate pleasure—taking a maiden properly for the first time.

He was smitten, and at her suggestion, pulled out of her and sat back on his throne and bid his men to unhand her. Free, Blanche turned, put her hands to her bodice and freed her breasts. Then she lifted up and came down into Simon's lap, positioning his cock herself with her own hands, and lowering her royal cunt on his staff—so that now it was he who was groaning and moaning and being controlled. None but I, I'm sure, saw her stealthily issue forth the vial of lamb's blood I

153

knew she kept in her bodice for any eventuality. And when he felt the blood run down his cock and heard her gasp and cry as she settled on him, who would call him a fool for believing he was deflowering a maiden who could not get enough of him and who valued his cocking so highly she was willing to give up a maidenhead that was worth gold and land?

I only had that fleeting glance, though, because as soon as Blanche was put in that first compromising position and her ass was being skewered, so was mine—and Kobus' as well. Other men in the hall were doing the same with us upon the table top that Simon was doing with Blanche.

To a large degree, though, the irony of this carefully orchestrated insult to the House of Lusane, was that it was a joke on Simon and his lot. Blanche was in her element and doing what she needed to do to survive. And both Kobus and I reveled in cocking by men. Beyond the sour smell and rough handling of the men poking us and nagging worry of what was to be done with us afterward, we both were enjoying the dominating fuck we were receiving. I often dreamed of lying with a nobleman, but nothing invigorated more than a soldier off the battlefield, celebrating that he still has a cock and lusting to punish, or a horse-hung peasant just in from the fields and in high rut.

Thanks to Blanche's guile, we all survived—although an inspection of our prison room when we returned to it, revealed that none of the handmaidens had escaped defilement in our absence either—multiple times. Through words of praise and endearment, Blanche convinced Simon that they would be so much more comfortable and aroused in his bed than here, and she convinced him to believe that such was his prowess Blanche did not want to leave his bed.

In this way, she saw to an improvement of the lot of all of us. And her quick wit also found a way to save us. Simon could use a secret supporter at the court of King Claude, could he not? Who better than someone who was a willing sex slave to him—and was the queen of the Kibrit court to boot? She would see to it that none of her retinue spoke of what really had happened in their captivity and, in turn, she would work for the survival of Limonea from within the Kibrit court.

How could Simon refuse, "knowing" how she melted to him as she did? And she had reminded him, in a cooing voice, that Kibrit was not that large of an island. That once the courts of Claude and Simon were in some sort of civil balance, there should be many an opportunity for Claude's queen to converse in private with Limonea's king. And while he thought on that, she sank before him and unlaced his codpiece and convinced him that no other cock pleased her as his did.

It had saved us, but at that moment in the Lefkosea castle courtyard and seeing the look Blanche was giving the vanquished king in his ox cart, I was wondrously thankful I was not Simon.

* * * *

In a formal ceremonial gesture, King Claude came down off the throne on the dais that had been set in the courtyard facing the gate arch under which, first, Rene and his officers, and then Simon's kingdom, his ox cart, and then rank on rank of the victorious soldiers, had entered. Then the king walked to a dismounting Rene, arms wide in welcome and hugged his young general and kissed him on each cheek. And at the very moment, after glancing at Rene's face and then quickly looking back into the face of my queen, Blanche, I saw that she saw what I saw.

This was still nothing to fault King Claude on concerning proper deportment or even acknowledged body urges. But it was not quite the same for Rene. Rene's eyes revealed his love for King Claude—and, more dangerously, even the nature of that love.

But here I think I part ways with Blanche. I had seen Rene before and had had time to think upon the sort of man he was—and to talk to soldiers about all three of them: Claude, Guy, and Rene.

I could understand the nature and extent of Rene's love and pining for Claude. I melted to both of them myself. But I believed I knew Rene as Blanche did not. I believe I knew that Rene, left unmolested, unchallenged, would have forever held to the high morality and a loyalty to his king that would not give Blanche challenge unless the king himself came to Rene.

Likewise with Claude I did not see that happening. In contrast to Blanche, though, of course, I saw the circumstances that prevented Claude and Rene from coupling as a tragedy rather than a noble necessity.

In Guy, though, I could see a vaulting ambitious and lust—and capability—that could take and control a king and queen simultaneously. And in this I was proved at least partially right.

In any event, Blanche set the whole thundering rattling of the world of Kibrit into motion by seeing a threat in Rene.

I was there, in the chamber, when she called her understeward, Kobus, to her. I was there when they discussed potions and means and effects. And I was there when she sent off the messenger, inviting Rene to celebrate his victory at Limonea and to thank him for her successful deliverance from captivity and the danger to the chastity of her and her handmaidens by visiting her chambers for a special meal on the morrow.

Rene could hardly refuse the invitation.

Blanche made the setting as innocently seductive as possible—and I was enlisted to aid in much of that. But the seduction was not for her personal use. She had far different plans for Rene.

The food served Rene was rich and the wine was heavy and full of flavor—full enough of flavor to hide any taste of the potion that was dropped into it.

Blanche served Rene herself. But she had help from Kobus in doing so. And as the meal moved on, Blanche was less in proximity to Rene and Kobus rather more.

The potion did not render Rene unconscious. It was quite an unusual and strong potion—it had been brought home from the crusades by her father. And Blanche believed in the power and effect of the potion, because, a castle crone having helped her, she had first used it on her father to erase all inhibitions of feeling first his tremulous fingers and then his tongue and then his cock delicately separating her nether lips and sliding inside her.

Rene did become a little woozy as the dinner progressed, but he also became more comfortable and more affable—and he smiled more and laughed more easily at the joking of Blanche and Kobus. At some point he was aware that Blanche declared that the king had sent for her to attend him in his chamber but that he should stay and finish the meal—that the seductively smiling understeward would see to his every need. But then she was gone and Rene thought of her no more.

He was beginning to think more about this sweet young understeward with the easy smile and the sensuous lips, and the fine lithe torso that Rene didn't quite remember having been bare when he started the meal. All of these brought to his mind his king.

And then the jokes became more intimate. And Rene found this funny too. And, yes, arousing as well. Kobus was sitting close beside him and feeding him grapes from his soft hands with the long, sinuous fingers.

Kobus was asking him if he had sustained any wounds in the battles for either St. Jerome or Limonea. And of course he had, as any warrior willing to ride into the thick of battle did. But just a few slash marks on his torso. He saw nothing out of the ordinary of Kobus wanting to see the wounds. And then, when his tunic had been removed, from wanting to touch them, to be reassured that they were mere hints of scars now on Rene's muscle-hard chest and belly, which of course they were.

And then the question of whether his muscles were sore and tight from battle and the hard ride north from Limonea seemed natural enough to ask, and the revelation that Kobus was trained in the art of massage sounded, in Rene's state, quite welcoming and innocent.

By the time that the muscle being massaged was the one between Rene's thighs and Kobus was doing the massaging with his mouth, Rene was lost to the attention. Emotionally, he had dreamed of this—and with the untouchable, with his king. Physically he'd had no idea of how wonderful it felt to be sucked by a man. And by such a young and seductive and beautiful man as Kobus.

Rene was in paradise when he was pushed down on his back on the fainting chase in the queen's antechamber and Kobus straddled his waist with his knees and positioned his channel on Rene's now-throbbing cock and gave Rene the first glorious male fuck of his life. I was not surprised to see what was now a lover's arrangement being solidified by, after a short period of rest, Kobus coaxing Rene to take the initiative and control and, more roughly and forcefully, to take the dominator's role in a second coupling, Kobus on his back, arms and legs splayed wide, and Rene pounding years of pent-up frustration between his thighs—accepting Kobus as a satisfactory substitute for who Rene really wanted to be doing this with.

I was there, in the chamber, for all of this. I watched it happen. I knew what it meant. I mourned the lost opportunity that it represented for King Claude and Rene, but I was proud of Blanche and her resourcefulness—and her determination to keep the king focused on producing a son and heir through her. That was her duty. That's what we had sailed from Holland and suffered diverse dangers and perils to accomplish. I was of the house of the Dutch, and the queen—my queen, was doing what she had to do to assure what she had been born to accomplish.

Rene was aware enough to know what Kobus was offering when he asked Rene if he wanted a companion in his bed for that night—and the night after.

Yes, of course he did.

I was in attendance in Rene's chamber, sent by the queen to provide her assurances of the success of her plan, to see a Rene in full control of his faculties fuck Kobus for hours in every conceivable position that Kobus could devise. And to release his seed repeatedly for the young understeward. Rene's unrequited lust for his king had been effectively neutralized.

I could truthfully return to the queen and assure her that Rene was smitten and that all of his attention was focused on the channel of a lover other than the king.

I did not fault Blanche, and I was pleased that Rene had found his true interest. But I did not trust Kobus and the overweaning ambition and mischievousness I saw in him. And, as it transpired, I did not trust him for good reason.

In high heat myself from what I observed, I went to Guido's chambers later that night and begged him to take care of me. But he didn't believe at first that I had anything to give him to make the act worth his while. I was forced to tell him of

Blanche's plan and that Rene had now declared and taken Kobus as his lover. I knew that Guido would go to Guy with this information and that Guy would become bolder, rightly considering the balance of power at court swinging in his direction. But I needed the release of the fuck, bent over a straight chair in Guido's chambers, the upward strokes pushing me up onto the balls of my feet with each swift thrust, that the information got me in reward for the disloyalty to my queen.

Chapter Four: Enter Trouble and Complication

All was at peace until, the kingdom of Turionia having been obliterated for all time by the heavy hand of the Duke of Gano, Guy and his forces, including Guido—and my channel still twitches at the thought of him—Guido returned to court in Lefkosea.

In Guy, Blanche, to her credit, saw a much more formidable and evil opponent than she had seen in Rene. The gazes he cast upon the king and the way he worked his way in between the thrones of the king and the queen in his counseling of the king, worried Blanche far more than anything else she had encountered in this strange island kingdom on the edge of the civilized world, where the warriors looked wilder and more bloodthirsty than any she had known on the continent and where their weapons were vicious and their manners unrefined. Blanche was to come to appreciate the wild-man weapons and rough manners of the local noblemen, of course.

She both did not like the look of domination and possessiveness that the overpowering and darkly handsome warrior duke cast on Claude, and, at the same time, she melted to it when turned her way. I watched Guy, seeing that he was assessing both the king and queen as avenues to influence and power. Such was his vanity—and his ability—that he almost managed both.

His chest was massive, his stride strong and self-assured, the pouch between his thighs bulging—and he had his breeches tailored to have the codpiece in contrasting color to emphasize that he was a horse and to be closefitting enough for the whole line of his pride to be followed by the eye.

Blanche was a queen, but she also was a woman and a hot blooded one at that. And try as he might and as beautiful as he was, the king's cocking was not fully satisfactory to her. She had taken a lover, one of the musicians in the king's small orchestra. He was a young man with a long and expressive tongue. She dare not go any further, and he did satisfy her for short periods with that talented tongue of his, but it had now been many months since a long, thick cock had worked inside her.

The Duke of Gano had the effect on her of both frightening her and arousing her. I watched her eyes go to that codpiece and saw it move and its contents thicken, as if on command, and I knew even then that the Duke of Gano would be riding the queen—if he wanted to. His demeanor when the king wasn't in evidence showed that he did want to and knew that he could if he wished.

At the same time, while understanding fully that the duke was a sensual, full-blooded man, Blanche also saw the interest he took in the king in matters that were much more than comradeship and fealty. What was this effect in her husband, she wondered, that set the juices of other men so? He, of course, had a beautiful body and was a king. But she had had better-endowed men of greater command in the bed. Could the reserve she felt in him when they were fucking have its roots in the attraction other men had for him? And did he know it? And did he feel the same way? She rather thought not, on both counts. At least for now. She thought perhaps that it was narcissism— that he was so beautiful and of such standing that he only had eyes for himself.

He looked at Guy with full openness, though, and Guy's grasping and calculating nature was equally honestly displayed. Blanche thought of someone like Guy with the throne's power, and she shivered at the vision. She decided she must see to it that it didn't come to that.

But why, she wondered, was it her lot that Claude was king and not Guy? Guy had a stable of sons—even several by the women he had married and buried. The rumor had gone through the court that Guy had a cock that wore women out and split them asunder. His manner of dress at court bore this out. To most of her maidens this was the stuff of fear and of trying to avoid his interest. But for Blanche, it set her heart thumping and gave her hot flashes.

What if, before Blanche could conceive and bear a son for Claude, that burning fire of sensuality that was the Duke of Gano achieved the attention of Claude. She was able to discern that Guy had the ambition and the desire and the appetite to gain complete sexual control over Claude if Claude permitted it. He certainly was showing the capacity to become more and more indispensable to Claude in matters of the kingdom.

She knew what Guido was to Guy too. Her spies were effective. She knew that, just as Guy had power to control with the cock, he could also be controlled with a youth's ass. And she knew of the instantaneous animosity that had sprung up between Kobus and Guido the day Guy and his entourage arrived at court. What if . . . what if the channel Guy plumbed at night was one devoted to the queen rather than to Guy?

She decided to divide and conquer—and to keep the king's men revolving around Claude in flux and uncertainty for as long as it took to produce an heir. Then she knew her power position would be solidified.

She decided to use Kobus once more.

And Kobus, having reasoned out the nature of Guido's control over me, decided to use me.

Thus it was that I, a silent, unseen fixture in the presence of the nobles at the Kibrit court, became instrumental yet again in their intrigues. I must admit, though, that it was neither the last nor the most significant moment that I passed over the stage of momentous events in the world of kings, queens, and dukes and found the spotlight, if only fleetingly, cast on me—or perhaps on the empty boards three paces from where I recently had been standing.

Kobus did not act directly. Through others he put out that I had a secret or two that Guy would like to know in his grasp for more and more power. And Kobus saw to it that this rumor reached the ears of Guido—and not just once nor from one source but from enough directions and frequency that it piqued Guido's interest. He had fucked useful secrets out of me before.

At the same time, the court being what it was, the rumors were running that the queen and Kobus were scheming something that affected Guy's standing.

Not those rumors alone either. The court in the dullness of peacetime was a snake pit of intrigue and gossip. Also, the tongue of the queen's musician became loosened with wine and with the bursting of pride of his special service to the queen, and this information too reached the ear of the duke.

Guy saw in that an opportunity. The beauty of the queen was not lost on Guy. His sexual drive knew no bounds and, although he had a special, deep longing for Claude, he was quite capable of enjoying a moist cunt as well—not to mention control of the influence the queen held.

In the weeks he'd been at court, he increasingly wondered about Blanche's cunt. Better networked abroad than even King Claude, he had heard rumors of Blanche's history with men and of her passion for big cocks. He had assumed she was no virgin when she came to Claude—but then all courtiers of intelligence in Lefkosea had assumed that as well. Except for trusting Claude, of course.

I was there on that afternoon as well—on the afternoon when, as Queen Blanche was walking the back passages of the castle from the women's wing to the queen's private garden— just me in attendance—Guy had materialized from the shadows—as I almost simultaneously shrank into them—and he took Blanche's arms roughly in his hands.

"What signifies this outrage, sir?" Blanche declared in a brave, yet tremulous voice. The mere presence of him so close to her set her breasts aching. "Unhand me and let me be on my way."

"You are not with child as yet, are you, your highness?" There was almost a sneer apparent in his voice.

"What is it to you?"

"After all these months, Claude's seed has not taken, has it? You are a smart woman. Have you not thought of what needs to be done about that?"

"You are too forward, Lord Guy."

"I also by-blow sons on alternate Fridays, my lady. Have you not thought of that? Have you not heard about and seen for yourself, the bow-legged stumbling of maidens and lads alike from my chambers with sloppy grins on their faces?"

She had. And there was nothing she could think to say about that. She was trembling almost uncontrollably. And Guy assumed—rightly—that very little of it was from fright.

"I have heard of your musician with the talented tongue, your highness. Did you think he would keep that tongue only for your entertainment? His tongue has been wagging about his privileged position at your girdle. The king may not have heard of it—and I can see that he doesn't. Although it will mean a permanent silencing of that tongue."

Blanche shuddered, knowing exactly what he was saying.

"But you would not miss such a tongue if it were replaced with a cock, would you? And not just any cock, but a cock such as I have. Surely you've heard of my cock, Blanche."

Blanche began to moan and to collapse in on herself. At this moment she was no longer a queen; she was a woman. Guy wrapped an arm around her waist, bringing her close into his body. He unlaced his codpiece, let the flap fall, and forced one of her hands below his waist. She gasped and moaned again, but she did not remove the hand when he lifted his hand free to cup her chin.

"And I know you have some other scheme afoot. I know not what it is, but I could reform it as the rumor revolves to sound like a plot against the king."

"You wouldn't," she cried out, the negative echoing down the canyon of the stone-walled corridor.

"And I have eyes and ears in courts as far away as Holland too. I know you like a fat cock. And now you have the measure of mine for your own. I know of your interest in horse-hung men and yet the king does not. Give a thought to how trustworthy I can be with your secrets—and how well I can fill that jewel purse of yours. Let us make a prince or three for the king, you and I, Blanche. There can be great pleasure in the serving of our king—for the both of us. Then all rumors in the kingdom will be stifled."

Blanche groaned, but she was still cupping his hard cock in her hand when he pushed her skirts up and roughly tore her undergarments away—and laughed when he felt her wet for him.

He laughed a hearty laugh again when it was Blanche's hands that guided his cock to plunging position. And when he swiftly filled and stretched her, riding her against the clammy stone wall, she encircled his hips with her legs and cried out in her passion of at long last—and perhaps as never before—being dominated and pumped by a cock far thicker and capable of reaching far deeper than Claude's did. When I saw his fat buttocks cheeks tighten and his body shudder and his head rear back with a roar to the ceiling, I also saw her tightly clasp her ankles behind his waist and beg him not to withdraw but, rather, to rest a bit and to do it again. I knew she was his, and my own heart shuddered at the thought.

A cock that could conceive a king. A man worthy of producing a king.

All of this I, a mere unseen, unremarked servant, observed and tucked away in my mind for further consideration.

* * * *

I am much grieved of my own part in what transpired between Kobus and Guido—and the misery and loss it marked for Rene and me. But I did what I could when I could to set that aright.

The queen's new plan was to use Kobus to neutralize Guy and to give her inside information on Guy's thoughts and schemes, and, in this, it became obvious that Guido needed to be removed.

The irony is that this was all set in motion and continued in motion as of itself before the queen took Guy as a lover and because the queen failed to inform Kobus of a change in circumstances.

Guy continued to meet the queen secretly and to fuck her silly, supposedly in their shared desire to produce a male heir for the king, but really, on Guy's part, to neutralize the power and scheming of the queen and on the queen's part because Guy had the thickest, strongest, longest, and most resilient cock she'd ever had inside her. And because he was a cruel lover. I never understood why women—or men, for that matter—often prefer a rough and cruel lover, but I can't deny that they do.

Come to think of it, I cannot deny that often I did as well.

That the queen never did produce a son in the natural sense or any daughters either, for that matter, probably spoke more of the capabilities of her womb than of the king's seed—and I never have heard of talk of a by-blow from Claude and don't expect ever to hear of one—than of the efforts of Guy. As it was, Guy, in his overweening vanity, probably would have assumed the son she did produce, like a rabbit out of hat, was his—if Guy had been alive when she produced that son.

Alas, I was the instrument of Guido's undoing, although that was the last momentous event—but one, which I shudder to think about—that happened outside my control. I may burn for what I write from henceforth of events if anyone sees this before I naturally die. But it is a story that needs to be told—if only to myself, so that I may fully appreciate what I have to account for in life. Besides, as feverish as I feel at this moment, what I write has my cock hard and standing straight and, from time to time, weeping quite pleasantly indeed. I regret that I did not write this all down sooner.

I did not knowingly or willingly undo Guido. To some extent he did it himself. The rumors that I knew things that would be very useful to his master, Guy, reached his ears and were repeated often enough for him to accept them as fact. And then he started to seek me out. I really had no idea that I was supposed to know anything—and I hardly thought it would help his master if what I told Guido was that his master was fucking my mistress, which he probably knew anyway, because, even if Guy wasn't sharing the information with Guido, Blanche was good enough at sucking the cum out of a man that Guido's channel was not being exercised as much now as it had been in the past by Guy's cock.

165

He thought I was teasing about not telling him the secrets. He tried bluster, but when that didn't work, he decided to try sex. He knew that that had worked in the past. The fucking worked wonders on me, but I still had nothing to tell him—and I was completely confused concerning why he was continuing to ask. The encounters had been furtive, brief couplings in nearly public areas, though. Guido reasoned that bedding me for a full night might be enough to loosen my tongue. I was delighted at the invitation, and his suggestion of using my small chamber in the queen's rooms was quite fine with me. So, the burden of the location chosen is on him, not on me. It was fully my mistake, however, of mentioning it to Kobus, seeking his help in keeping a private time for Guido and me.

This was the opportunity Kobus had been waiting for.

I was on my back on my cot, in the near-total darkness Guido had demanded, my legs open to Guido, who, after a first coupling with me bent over the cot, and, he behind me, had, gloriously, taken us both down together in an entangled, heavy-breathing unity on the cot and slept briefly there as I regained my breath and he regained his stamina. He whispered his questions in my ear, and I tried my best to think of what I might tell him that he wanted to hear. Taking my reaction as coyness, he sighed a deep sigh of resignation and turned me on my back and presented himself between my raised and spread legs. I was in heaven. He was mining me deeper and for longer than I'd ever had before, when he gave a little cry and collapsed on me and I felt the handle of the knife buried between his ribs and the wetness of his blood.

Kobus was standing over the cot, a gleam of victory in his eyes, completely unfeeling of the shock and extreme despair I felt. Guido had been right. I was attractive to almost no man. He was a god among men. But even knowing he fucked me to control me, I loved him because he fucked me. And that was all the world to me.

"I have men outside. They will take care of the body," Kobus was whispering. I only half heard him, still deep in trauma myself. The body was still lying on top of me. His cock was still hard inside me. I whimpered at the feel of it shriveling up inside me, knowing I would never feel its hardness again.

"You clean the room. Leave not a trace of him or his blood. The body will completely disappear. No one will know what happened."

As Guido's lifeless body was being taken off me, I felt his cock leaving me. For the last time. I waited until I was alone. And then I curled into a ball on the cot and cried like a baby. Later in the night, when I had done everything that Kobus instructed me to do, I sat on the floor of my chamber—in a corner as far away from the cot as I could—and as I rocked my enfolded body back and forth and my tears continued to flow, I began to scheme on my own.

I may have been invisible—almost a nonperson—to these noblemen with their intrigue and treacheries, but I was not powerless. And I determined then to make my own mark on the court of the island kingdom of Kibrit.

Within a week, Guy, showing only slight pique at Guido's disappearance and rather more frustration at the absence of his channel, had learned of Kobus' massage skills and experienced Kobus' talents at massaging his cock and had taken Kobus into his bed.

Kobus assumed that, like he had done with Rene, his service to the queen was to keep Guy from coupling with the king and to be her eyes and ears in Guy's bedchamber. What he didn't know—and never learned, because he himself was not long for this world—was that the queen was preoccupied with Guy's cock and mastered by his control now herself and no longer greatly cared who did or did not couple with the king.

Rene despaired the loss of Kobus in his bed, and in that loss, now, once again turned his eyes on the king. The difference now was that Rene knew the glories of churning in a man's channel. He knew far more now both about his affection for the king and about what that entailed than he had at the fall of St. Jerome.

And what I knew was that the king probably wanted what Rene had to give, even though he did not realize it—and that Rene deserved to have his chance with the king.

I also knew that both Guy and Kobus had to go. I was too genetically loyal to the queen to give any similar thought to her.

Chapter Five: By the Switching of the Cup

It was Blanche who gave me the courage and confidence to do what I did. It is true that I gained the necessity to do something because I watched her going under the control of the Duke of Gano's cock and, having seen what he could do and was willing to do, I despaired of the whole kingdom coming under his sway.

Until now, although Blanche's schemes had served her, they also had served the House of Lusane.

I had no idea that I might be trusted and brought into one of Blanche's schemes as the clever and resourceful Kobus had been. But that she trusted a task as sensitive and significant to me as she did opened my eyes to my own possibilities.

After several months of moving almost in one continuous line between the king's bed and the duke's bed, Blanche's womb had not quickened and there was no sign of a child baking inside her. She knew this couldn't go on; she had promised a son by summer and it already was early spring. And although she didn't take the blame on herself, the blame was not what was needed—especially if anyone suggested that it might lie with the king. What was needed was a male child.

She called me forth to her writing desk one sunny morning in early April and smiled at me and said, "Before Christmas time I will give King Claude a son."

"Oh, my lady," I muttered, my eyes opening wide, feeling a heavy cloud lifting off us all.

"And you are going to provide the baby," she went on, looking at me levelly.

I felt a hand squeezing around my heart and my cock and balls shriveling. Was this some kind of joke? She knew what I was. If the king and the randy duke together couldn't impregnate her, how was she expecting me to do it?

"It was Agnes. My handmaiden, Agnes. who gave me the idea. She was quickened back while we were under Simon Limona's care. I'm surprised not more of the maidens were."

"But my lady, I don't understand. Surely you aren't suggesting . . . a child of some Limonean soldier?"

"No, no. We have taken care of her inconvenience. But it gave me an idea—and then a plan."

"A plan, my lady?"

"Yes a plan. And you are key to the plan. You can be out and about as no one else in my retinue but Kobus can. But Kobus is almost chained to Guy's bed now." I could hear the bitterness and female jealousy in her voice over that, even though she had been the one to set the plot in motion that put Kobus there. She continued, however, "He has no ability to do what I need done."

"And what is that, my queen?"

"I need to have a baby—no two—growing. They need to be of noble Kibrit lineage, of course. That goes without saying. But they need to be an inconvenience to the noble family they are budding inside."

"I don't know how I can—"

"Shush. I will tell you how you can. First you will go into the court and listen to the gossip. I know you do that anyway. I've seen you. You think you move about invisibly. And you may do so with most at court. But not with me. I know that you know far more than any one person at court does about what is going on inside our little village here. And I know that all gossip at some point passes to you. I am equally sure that it stops with you. And that is why I am giving you this task. This is perhaps the most important task I have given anyone."

Suddenly I felt important. I almost felt like I was a person.

"I want you to identify two maidens in need of a quiet disappearance of a baby. I know this is usually handled by ending the child's life before birth or finding a second- or third-ranked family with the need for another set of hands in the field or in service. But I need two on contract. Two because it must be a son, and this strengthens the possibility of that. And then this is what I want to be arranged—that I want you to arrange, and in total secrecy."

She went on, me attempting hard to tune to her but all aflutter inside because of the euphoria she had infused me with on the mere trust in assigning the task.

But I did well—at least in what Blanche commanded me to do. One of the maidens of a noble family I made secret arrangements with did, indeed, bear a son. The other child was stillborn, which solved the issue of having two sons available. But the family with the new fatherless son was delighted to know that their lineage would be sitting on the throne of Kibrit, even though they presently couldn't gain from that knowledge and must keep it a secret.

What Blanche did not know, however, was that I took longer than I need have, there being much boredom and therefore much dalliance in the court of Kibrit after the island had been consolidated under one rule. And the reason I took longer was that I went to great pains to assure myself that the chosen baby was not a by-blow of Guy de Gano. That proved to be a much harder undertaking than I had supposed it would be.

As fall moved into winter, Blanche started to show and to glow. She was a magnificent actress. All were duped—well, not all. Three of us beside Blanche and a few select of her handmaidens knew she was not with child and that the deception was being promoted by subtle uses of clothing and padding and cosmetics.

King Claude was no problem. He was told that the queen could not accommodate him during the lying-in time for fear of the safety of the child. He took the news well enough, visibly with relief, actually, concentrating on the excellent news that Blanche at last had conceived. He then gladly contented himself with hunting and warrior training with Rene, Guy, and a group of his younger officers. That Claude found this more stimulating than trying to impregnate his wife did not occur to Claude as a function of his greater interest in the shape of a man's body than a woman's—but that would come in time.

Guy was a problem. First, he did not buy the delicacy of the baby-in-the-womb argument for one moment. He had fucked women into their eighth month at least and knew the positions that made that both possible and enjoyable. Well, enjoyable for him, at least, which was all that mattered to him. And, perhaps more important, because he had no paucity of cunts or asses to dip his cock in, he knew his hold over Blanche was sexual—that given too much time off from his cocking, she was likely to separate from him and become the strong political force she had been before he subdued and dominated her.

Although she declared that she was in her fourth month already and therefore would only attend the court occasionally and would withdraw to the mountain castle at St. Jerome for her health and that of her child, Guy rode to her there in the dark of night, stormed into her chamber, swept both her guards and her handmaidens aside, and rode her as hard as he'd ridden his horse to get to her.

Blanche took him lustfully, being a complete slave to his staff and all the more impassioned because he had stormed the castle and breached her defenses to get to her and had taken her hard and rough like a conquest of battle. But when he felt for the mounding he knew should be there at this point—and that rather increased than stemmed his ardor for a woman when he knew he had fucked that child into her womb—he found none. And having found none, he had to be told the truth of it and the reason for it.

Both Kobus and I were in the room, standing invisible to the couple in the bed, of course. So, of men knowing the truth of it, there was Kobus and me . . . and Guy.

I knew that Guy would use the knowledge and would do so in ways that would split the tranquillity of Kibrit asunder.

Blanche had entrusted me to see to the creation of a king. Even though she was so besotted with Guy that I could not discuss the matter with her, I knew that she could trust me to ensure the rule of that king. I knew that once she was freed of the domination of Guy's cock, she would thank me for what I then did—for the good of the kingdom.

* * * *

"Should there not be a great ball at court to celebrate the coming of this child, my queen?"

"What?" she responded to me as we sat in the belvedere of St. Jerome and I peeled a pomegranate for her. "A ball?"

"Yes, I'm sure the king would have thought of it if he was not occupied with the sighting of unknown war ships off Papheas. But there is no reason why you could not command it?"

"And for what purpose?"

"Is not the coming of an heir purpose enough—and the court seeing you dressed and showing for the part?"

"Yes, yes, perhaps it is," she answered.

And thus began the unfolding of my second-to-most bold plot.

Fortuitously, Kobus, as understeward and confidant to the queen, was the keeper of her potions—and everyone at court knew that, because that was the natural function of an understeward. And equally fortuitously I was able to gain access to these potions without the knowledge of either Kobus or the queen and, in those moments of being just another salamander on the wall, I had followed their making of potions and learned what each one of them was for.

This knowledge—all of it—was important to me because it was not just Guy, Duke of Gano, I was targeting, for the good of the kingdom, but it was also Kobus, for my own purposes. He had murdered the man I loved, Guido, even while he was working his magic inside me. This had continued to fester in my breast. I needed vengeance against Kobus to stem my grief and satiate my, by necessity, barely contained anger.

I started with my plan in the queen's antechamber, among her handmaidens. I separately went to the most empty-headed and loose tongued of them and casually slipped into otherwise innocuous conversations the question of whether the queen's relationship with the duke could possibly be a source of jealousy for Kobus, who the queen herself had placed in the duke's bedchamber.

And then I sat back and waited. Six days before the great celebration banquet of the queen's pregnancy, I began to hear the rumors come back at me—deepened and coarsened—in the gossip chain. I was very, very pleased with myself.

At the same time, I started working on Kobus, telling him that I had seen Rene, now free of Kobus' ministration, fucking the king and connecting it with the king's announcement raising Rene to the status of duke over the former city state of Limonea and the lands surrounding it in the south of Kibrit. The ascension was no more than his due, of course, but I had seen the effect of this on Guy, Duke of Gano—and now of the former region of Turionia as well. The king had announced both new ranking simultaneously and his actual action was well balanced, of course, but with a little help of the gossip chain, which I supplied, and my more direct talk of a new bedroom arrangement between Rene and the king to Kobus, Guy was quite prepared to see everything as balanced against him, and the portent of serious storm clouds on the horizon.

Kobus had no idea how to help Guy in this matter. By happenstance I did. In this instance, I didn't even have to mix the poisonous potion. Kobus quite willingly did it with his own hands.

All I had to do was, at the most strategic moment, switch who got the cup of poison at the high table during the great celebration. What was once Rene's to drink became Guy's to gag and die from.

In the aftermath, more than one courtier was quite happy to say that they had seen Kobus poison Guy's cup—and nearly the whole court could put a name to the reason why.

I didn't mix that potion, but I did mix the one that Kobus took in prison and begged me for because of the gruesomeness of the punishment that had been ascribed for the crime of killing a duke.

* * * *

Although I could have left it at that, I was heady from my new-found power over the world of the nobility, and I could not get out of my mind the tragedy of the king and Rene so obviously loving and wanting each other and neither being about to step over the boundary of duty and propriety—especially when all of those around them at court, including the queen, showed no knowledge whatsoever of the existence of such a boundary. I wasn't the only one to have observed the king and Rene pining ineffectually for each other, and increasingly I heard the whispers of folks both noting the brazenness of the foreign queen Blanche and hinting that they wished that the king and Rene just got on with it. Blanche was not loved at court. And now that she was fulfilling her duty to provide a son, those at court were more dismissive of her needs and increasingly concerned for the happiness of their king. Those of Kibrit truly were on the margin of civilization. To them, a hole was a hole, and satisfaction, no matter how derived, was the goal.

Since I had saved his life—and since he had a body that made me want to withdraw into a corner and pleasure myself—I started to serve Rene as often as I could. I found myself in his presence after a hard hour or two of practice on the sword field with the king and the other young king's men—which, in all honesty, I enjoyed watching anyway, because, when they were working with wooden swords, they practiced in just breechcloths and the movement of their lithe, well-muscled bodies was very pleasing to me. It was less nerve-racking for me to watch the practices now than before, when Guy also was on the practice field and exuded power and sensuality and foreboding.

The men engaged in bouts of wrestling too in these practice sessions to keep their reflexes quick and their bodies supple for close-in combat. It had been when I watched the king wrestling with either Guy or Rene that I realized that he was overripe for the plucking by either one and that it would only be a matter of time before one or the other speared him with their shaft, with then the inevitable unbalancing of the weight of influence the two very different counselors had on the king. I assessed the king as a true romantic, who would be constant to one lover and could as easily be dominated by that lover as complemented. As strong a field commander and temporal king as he was, I could see that, as with me, the king wanted to be commanded and dominated in bed.

Guy was definitely the dominator. He was aggressive and powerful, and the atmosphere of a wrestling bout between him and the king was one of a battle for control to the death, if necessary. When the king was wrestling with Rene, it was a beautiful dance of strategy and positions and holds in which each remained equal and in balance, with Rene slightly on the ascendance. The latter was more pleasant to watch, but I feared the implications of the former. As far as I could tell, the king had no preference between the two as long as he was being controlled.

In both cases, I watched the king carefully and am surprised that no one else saw what I did—that he was receptive to and aroused by either of his lieutenant's approaches to the grappling, to the struggle of ascendance. Not only could I see the tenting of his breechcloth and the hooding of his eyes, and the response of his nipples to what could equate to the groping of Guy or the fondling of Rene, but I could also see that he melted to the controlling embrace of either and that, as he slowly—more from mental choice than physical necessity—let himself be controlled and subdued—something he permitted of no others than Guy and Rene. In his wrestling matches with these two, as he slowly let himself be overmatched, I could see him positioning himself for mounting, wanting it at least subconsciously if not in his surface cognizance. And I think that, at those times, if they had not been in the public field, among his soldiers, he himself would have taken the initiative at that point, perhaps not knowing he had but not drawing away once he had.

And knowing both Guy and Rene, I knew that at that point Guy would have fucked the king mercilessly and Rene lovingly—and that the king would have enjoyed either fully and would have been lost to either then as a lover.

Perhaps I was able to see this as no others could because I was the same with the king in what I wanted and how the effect of being in the presence of Rene—and, yes, Guy too—made me ever ready to position myself for mounting as well.

I am certain Guy never had the king, but I do know of a time that it became a close thing. One afternoon, as the court was in full preparation for the queen's ball, he had appeared at the queen's chamber door in high heat. I, unfortunately, had to inform him that the queen was then with a messenger departing in a short time for Holland and that she was writing messages to her family that would have to be sent off almost before she could complete them. Guy was in high flush and his eyes were wild in that way of men with cum built up that must be spilled. I could sense his mind grinding away, and I knew almost as soon as he did that the visage of the queen in his mind was being replaced by that of the king. They had wrestled the previous day, and I saw then that Guy fully understood what I knew—that if they had not been on the public field, that all Guy would have had to do was pull away his breechcloth and thrust inside the king and he would have had the king in thrall to him not only in the bedchamber but in the council chamber as well.

I knew Guy had been ruminating on this and that this is why he was in such high heat. And I knew it was a mistake—although completely unavoidable—to tell him the queen's jewel box was not presently free and open to him. I knew as surely as he did that the king was now prepared to give him in private what he could not give him in public the previous day—not just a fuck but also the keys to the kingdom.

In terror, I followed along behind him as he wheeled around and made straight for the king's private chambers. It must have been the gods who had intervened, because, in transit, Guy went by an archway looking out onto the king's garden. There, posed prettily on a balcony wall, was a young, comely Italian page, stripped down to his breechcloth and arching his back to take in the sun. If I had been a man who cocked men, I couldn't have resisted the delectable confection myself. In Guy's explosive state, he couldn't either. He had the lad leaning precariously out over the abyss, his legs slapped aside, Guy's hands clutching his waist, and his cock forcing its way home in a trice. The obviously virginal young page yowled shock, violation, and pain, all of which only exploded Guy's arousal and need for instant gratification. The youth kept on yowling, not knowing that this only egged one such as the cruel duke on, and Guy kept on thrusting with his hips with all his considerable might until all of his pent-up sexual tension and fury and a flood of cum had been spent inside a moaning page on a balcony in the king's garden.

I tended to the babbling heap the page had become when Guy finished with him and strode back toward his own rooms. I was sympathetic to the lad, but I had to bite my lip not to inform him that he very likely had saved an empire.

Four days later the duke was dead. It was obvious that he had to go.

After that, it was only Rene on the practice field who was wrestling with the king and having the melting affect on the king that only I seemed to be able to see. There was still tension now, but it was not one I thought of as a danger to the kingdom; it was one of "when will this stop; when will they ever get on with it?" I thought that Rene was as much the problem as the king, and I resolved, after a practice where I could see both were panting for it and neither making the strategic move, to give Rene the little push he needed. When he came away from practice, I was there to help him bathe and then, after I told him I was trained in massage, I was permitted to become more intimate with his body with my hands.

After weeks of slowly getting more intimate with my hands working the muscles of his body, Rene felt moved and comfortable enough with going to full erection when he was turned on his back. And then, he became comfortable with having me in the chamber alone with him when I massaged him. And having my mouth massaging his cock.

He never fucked me where I longed to have his cock working, but it was not long before he was sending for me to give him a massage rather than me following him around and asking him if he wanted one.

To my knowledge he had never replaced Kobus in his bed, when Kobus displaced Guido in Guy's bed. But I made known to myself that there was no physical reason why he could not easily reach an erection or produce a prodigious amount of cum out of a very nice, long, and plump cock.

"Why is it, sire, that you never have had a lover since Kobus?" I boldly asked one day when I had sucked him dry during a massage and then found that he wanted me again before I had finished working his muscles.

"I don't do it lightly, Lambert," he said. "And I will not do it for you, if that is why you are asking."

"No, sire, it is not. I know that one such as I could not aspire to one such as you. You have a cock suitable for a king."

He stiffened then, and I heard his ragged intake of breath.

"The king, sire," I pressed further. "Why is it that you never have lain with the king?"

"You presume, servant," he said angrily.

"I feel how you stiffen at the mention of his name," I persisted. "I see how you look at him, how you watch him, your gaze going lovingly over the curves of his body, lost in the deep, soft blue of his eyes. Your cock stiffens at the sight of him on the practice field, the hardness of his muscles, the fullness of his lips, the way the world lights up when he smiles at you, the blondness of his curls. The way that line of hair runs down under the hem of his breechcloth. The blondness of his bush. I know as we have both been there when he bathed. The plump roundness of his nether cheeks, the curve of his cock up from his belly. The blush of his bulb, its slit ripe for a tongue or a probing finger. And I feel the engorging of your cock at my lips even as I say these things."

"Oh, God, enough," he cried out, and he stopped my speech with his cock plunging up between my waiting lips and pumping, pumping, pumping in a frenzy until he ejaculated and his muscles relax and he collapsed on the divan.

"I ask again, sire. Why have you never lain with the king? You want to."

"Because he doesn't want me." It came out as a strangled cry. "If he did, he would command."

"There you are wrong, sire. I see how he looks at you, how his eyes follow you on the practice field and even in the supper hall. He very much wants you. But he needs what you need."

There was no immediate response from Rene, and in exasperation, I blurted out, "The king commands in the field and in temporal matters—and he does it superbly. But the king is such a man as to want another man to command him in the bed. I've watched him. His eyes are on you to command him in the bedchamber. His channel aches for your cocking. He wants what you gave Kobus." Glory be, I thought, that I didn't have to tell him that the king would have taken Duke Gano's command in the bedchamber as easily as Rene's and that it was only by my plotting and hand that Rene's reluctance and naiveté were not to be his undoing.

"You said he needs what I need. What did you mean by that?" the question was an anguished whisper.

"He needs a first time."

"I have waited for years," Rene sobbed. "There are no first times with this king for a man laying with a man. He is a king."

"He is first and uppermost a man. You do him no service by holding him beyond reach when he obviously aches for you so. There was a first time with you and Kobus," I whispered. "And that only happened because Kobus, the queen, and I made it so."

"What are you saying?"

"Did you regret having Kobus as a lover?"

"No. No, of course not."

"Neither would the king regret having you as a lover. I know this is so. And I know it is right. And not just for the two of you, but for the kingdom."

"Explain yourself. About Kobus and me that first time."

"Do you not remember being in a haze?" I asked. I was slowly stroking his cock with my hand now, bringing him back to arousal in body to bring him back to arousal in mind as well.

"Yes. But I was tired and it was the drink."

"Not those entirely, no. Not those to an extent where it counted. There was a potion. An otherwise harmless potion."

"A potion? A . . . yes, yes, Lambert. That, with your hand. I could . . . all day. Oh, god yes."

"And you could be doing it with the king," I whispered. "Yes, a potion. Do you remember how you felt? Was Kobus desirable to you? Was his touch electric? Did you feel all of the power and strength of you flowing to your hard cock? Did your inhibitions against doing what your body clearly wanted lessen?"

"Yes, and yes," Rene answered.

"It was the potion. I have the potion."

"The massage. It was so arousing. Not unlike your massages."

"I dare say you can massage the king as well as Kobus or I ever did you. But hush, now, and think further on this at your leisure. I can help you. But for now, I feel you tightening up. I feel it in your orbs. For now my hands and lips have other work

179

to do here. For this information, I only ask for the honor to drink of you."

* * * *

I was there, in the chamber, unseen and unmarked, as always, although in full view for anyone who wanted to see me, who needed my assistance, when the king and the king's man first fucked.

It was in the evening, their suppers on tables beside their chairs, the chairs turned three quarters to each other to ease conversation—and, because I had set them—to enhance the view of each other. They had been out hunting, the king and all the king's men, his lieutenant, Rene, at his side the entire time.

They had ridden back exhausted, but happy. This peacetime interlude in their lives was more taxing on a warrior than battles were. It was harder to keep their bodies hard and supple. Neither the king nor Rene need worry about that for some time to come, though.

They had been cleaned—I had helped with both, my hands working efficiently, making sure the king felt my touch on his cock and shuddered at the seemingly innocent arousal it provided. The two of them talking to each other of the crusade the king had pledged to join. Both happy, both seeing an end coming to this dull peacetime.

They were sitting in the chairs, talking and supping and drinking, only in their loosely laced breechcloths. Comfortable with each other. Long-time friends. Total trust between them.

They were both cleaning and sharpening their swords. No servant was ever allowed to do this for a knight. None could be trusted to do this just right.

The king was complaining about the discomfort of his new boots. They hadn't been crafted just right. He rose and walked over and sat on the end of his enormous, high-postered bed and began to take his boots off.

He had been weaving a bit as he walked, and Rene looked hard at me, perhaps fully seeing me there for the first time.

Yes, I am the one who prepared his drink, I signaled with the expression of my face and hands. And then I nodded and leaned my head toward the king, sitting on the end of his bed.

Rene cleared his throat. "You look tired and tense, my king," he said.

"I am. I should not have foregone the hunt earlier in the week. My muscles complain of it from today's outing. This lack of the demands of battle vex me; I must exercise more."

If I have my way, you will exercise vigorously at night, I thought as I drifted into the shadows.

"May I send for a man to give you a massage?" I could have slapped Rene then for this clumsy approach in this question—volunteering to bring a substitute into the chamber—but the king did not fall in that direction.

"No bother. It is minor. They all will be at their supper now and will do a begrudging job, even though I be king."

"Then perhaps . . . I"

"You?"

"Yes perhaps just the shoulders if you feel that might suffice."

"Well . . ."

Rene was kneeling on the bed behind the king, close to him, his hands working the king's shoulders. Claude was rotating his head on his neck and Rene moved his hands to where the skull and neck joined, dug in his fingers gently, and the king let out a long, satisfied sigh.

Rene worked the bicep muscles and then returned to the shoulders briefly. I could see the king relaxing. And I could see something else as well. The crotch of his breechcloth was tented and I could see the bulb of his cock at a slit in the cloth. He could feel the need of Rene in the small of his back. I could tell that for sure. His eyes were hooded and he was panting in short, shallow breaths. I could see the muscles of the king's flat belly knotting. Rene's hands came down onto the king's chest and he was massaging the king's chest muscles, running his fingers over and over the king's now-taut nipples.

It was Claude who made the first, decisive move. I applauded him for that, and I was grateful. Rene was the perfect subject, awaiting the command, to the end in that first coupling. I was despairing of him making an irrevocable declaration openly acknowledging the need, the want, the repressed intention of both.

Rene was looking down the line of Claude's torso, seeing for the first time that the breechcloth had fallen away and that Claude was in full, upward curved erection, arising from his golden bush. At that moment, before Rene could decide what, if anything to do next, Claude raised his face to Rene's and captured Rene's lips with his. The kiss was tentative at first, but then they both hungrily opened to each other, as of a beaver's piling being swept away by a torrential rain.

Rene cupped the king's chin in one hand, keeping their kiss going. The other hand slid down the king's torso along the line of blond, curly hair, down his belly and through his golden bush and captured the king's cock. Almost as if this bold action jolted him, though, Rene started to take his hand away. Claude covered it with one of his own hands, though, and one or the other of them started the slow masturbation of the royal shaft.

The kiss broke and the king whispered something to Rene and Rene whispered back, and then I saw the king stand from the bed and bend completely and grab his ankles. Rene went into a sitting position behind him, and his lips went into the fold of the royal rump. I moved around the room to make sure, and then satisfied myself that one of Rene's hands had moved between Claude's thighs and had resumed the milking of the royal cock.

It was the king who made the move of rising and then sitting in Rene's lap, half skewering his channel on Rene's cock. The king didn't come all of the way down, though. He crouched over Rene's lap and fucked himself slowly on Rene's staff using the traction of the balls of his feet on the floor. It was still the king's choice.

Rene was palming the king's belly with both hands and moaning deeply. In truth they were both moaning.

I walked to them then and sank between their spread knees and took the king's cock in my mouth. He didn't even seem to realize I was there, but he didn't command me away, and his enjoyment of the experience seemed to increase, if the intensity of groans and sighs from both was any measure.

When the royal seed hit the back of my throat, I took it as my due, my reward. As none of this would have happened without my boldness or persistence. In years hence they would both assume they just found each other, I am sure. This is how histories are written. But I knew that it had taken far more than that.

I felt the moment when Claude's body shuddered and Rene's first flow inside the king bathed the royal channel.

I pulled back into the shadows as Rene drew the king up on the bed. They lay there for some time, bodies stretched against each other, hands roaming, whispering to each other.

And then, at a whisper from Claude, Rene was turning the king on his belly and mounting his hips. And riding to paradise.

They did this through the night, finding and loving new positions, solidifying their new life as lovers, and making Rene the true king's man. There still, at the back of my mind, though, was some reservation over what was transpiring.

Toward dawn they settled down in each other's arms and I curled up in the shadows of a corner and slept as well.

I awoke to the sounds of groaning. Rene was sitting on the foot of the bed. The king was crouched between his legs, his mouth covering as much of Rene's cock as possible. Rene's hips were rolling in a slow rhythm that had his cock pushing as far into Claude's mouth as he could take it. The king was gagging, but he would not give up the cock.

I saw Rene bending over the king's bare back, reaching for and achieving a grip on the king's buttocks cheeks with his large, battle-callused hands. He squeezed the orbs and then, with a laugh, he slapped each in succession. He squeezed them again and spread them wide, and I saw the tips of the middle finger of each hand push into and spread apart the opening to the king's channel, the rim of which was rosy red from the previous nights cocking. Claude wiggled his rump but continued sucking Rene's cock.

Suddenly, Rene was aroused beyond control, and he stood and held the king away from him with hands on the king's arms. He turned the king's body and slammed it down on the surface of the bed. Claude arched his back and his head and I heard him laugh with a deep, joyful laugh, as Rene laced his arms under the king's thighs, spread and raising the monarch's legs, and knotted his hands on the king's belly. The bulb of his cock was positioned at Claude's entrance. He pushed the bulb a few inches inside and rotated it, while Claude gasped and groaned. Then he slid fast and deep inside as Claude cried out his passion. The king was panting and groaning and babbling of the master taking when I silently left the room. Rene's cock was giving him no quarter, strongly and cruelly slamming inside the royal hole again and again and again.

I was satisfied. This was what I had been waiting to see—the two taking their natural roles in the bedchamber. Rene taking dominating command as the king wanted him to.

Weeks later, King Claude and Duke Rene left on a crusade to Jerusalem. Claude did not take Blanche with him, leaving her on Kibrit as regent of the kingdom.

Blanche was content in raising the crown prince. As the prince grew older, I realized that I had failed terribly in one aspect of my scheming. The prince was growing up looking the spitting image of Guy, Duke of Gano. Blanche no doubt was happy with this. I had my serious doubts.

Before Claude and Rene returned from their crusade, I had had enough of scheming and plotting among the nobility and had requested and been granted by Blanche—no doubt now seeing me as a loose end that had seen entirely too much—permission to withdraw to the house of the brothers near Papheas to live out my years in contemplation.

Chapter Six: Fini

My first reaction was to laugh when I'd reread what I'd written. Remembering it now, my "secret" potion for Rene in loosening up the king to his maddeningly tentative advances was a combination of very good brandy, honey, and sugar water. I had no idea what Kobus and Blanche had put into the potion they'd given Rene—or even if it was any more "magical" than what I had given the king for Rene. It had been a gamble, but my own view had turned out a winner. The king only needed to be started in giving himself to Rene—and then Rene only needed a little push once beyond the vale himself in sensing his true role in their couplings. The only potion he had needed was confidence, bravery, and brashness—traits that Guy de Gano had had in full, I'm afraid. It would have been best for all if it had been the other way around. Guy might even have kept his life then.

The laugh, though, caused me to cough and for a pain to run through my chest like a fist had gripped my heart. And it made me think upon what I had written with greater introspection. I had always believed that we servants of the nobility were invisible and of no consequence. After letting all of this story pour out on parchment, the complete truth of it as I had witnessed and lived, I could still believe in the invisibility. But I couldn't believe in the lack of consequence in the presence of servants.

In consolidation of the House of Lusane on the island of Kibrit and its first crucial months of life, the nobles had schemed and intrigued, yes, but many of the momentous events—and some of the most spectacular ones—had been initiated and carried through by the unseen servants.

I have no regrets about the acts that my own hands performed in events save not having kept Guido out of harm's way and not being careful enough to find a princeling who had not been sired by Guy—which would have required a miracle.

But also now that I reread this, I realize that it is too volatile to ever be seen. I can't save and hide this someplace. If this fell into the wrong hands, into the hands of Blanche's enemies at court, to be specific—and there are many—the House of Lusane might be undone. Of course it could as easily be strengthened as to unravel and fall into dust.

But I came to Kibrit as Blanche's servant and she has let me live and enjoy life here among the monks—some of whom, I am happy to say, have nice cocks and aren't too picky—when it might have been more in her interest to have me dispatched while she was regent. She ruled for Claude for five years while he and Rene were on their crusade. And she ruled rather heavy-handedly, more as a foreign occupier than a Kibrit queen. For this she was resented deeply at court, and a great sigh of relief was sounded when King Claude and Duke Rene rode back into the castle forecourt at Lefkosea. Not a word of reproach was gossiped about when the two men moved directly into the same bedchamber, as grateful were the people of the island that they had returned. I'm sure that his subjects assumed that at least Claude was dominant in that chamber, and I've never heard a hint to the contrary. This most likely means that the king's and king's man's chamber servants are far more discrete than I was able to be.

Blanche quickly retired to the bastion at St. Jerome to enjoy the company of an assortment of men who visited her there. Although she reappeared at court for high celebrations and relations between her and the king were quite proper, neither objected to or sought to change the choices each had made for their lives.

Blanche took the crown prince with her—and the entire court breathed a sigh of relief. I would not dare write of the crown prince if I had not now already decided what must be done with this true, bald, and unvarnished history I've written. But the boy was a brat, demanding and mischievous, and promised, in visage, to grow handsome and troublesome and completely self-centered and self-possessed and to scheme deaths and break hearts and create an army of by-blows—every inch his true father. And if this history reached the wrong hands, I can clearly see that it would be my mistress's undoing. Already I've heard talk in the land of Claude naming Rene his successor—even of adopting him formally.

So, I know what I must do with this parchment, burning its unmentionable truths in the palms of my hands as I hold it before me—in a moment when my heart stops beating so wildly. Perhaps I am getting too old to seek out stable boys' and monks' cocks. I cannot remember needing so long to catch my breath and have my heart return to its regular rhythm.

Just a brief rest and I will stir up the fire and take this parchment and . . .

~

Dirk Hessian

An artist and writer, Dirk has always been interested in history and legends, particularly those of the United States, the Mediterranean, and Asia. His works are historical, and sometimes border on fantasy. They are full of ordinary men struggling to survive and find love in difficult situations. And sometimes Dirk writes about men who are in touch with forces beyond those of mortal men, fighting for survival in more unusual ways.

Dirk's books often, but not always, contain male sex that is both forceful and rough, and at times dangerous, but is always within the context of stories of survival in more primitive and brutal times. He also writes about the power of love in turbulent times.

He can be found at the adults only gay male site www.BarbarianSpy.com, which he shares with Sabb and habu (sr71plt).

Our authors always like to receive feedback, and appreciate it when readers post reviews to Goodreads, Amazon, B&N, Smashwords and other review sites.

BarbarianSpy

FOR LITERARY HEAT

Not all books listed below may currently be on release.
* indicates the book is available in paperback and e-book.

BOOKS BY CHRIS CROSS
Multisexual Adult Romance
Pulaski Square
Chocolate in Vanilla (MF)
Christmas with Chris (MMF) (MM) (MF)

BOOKS BY ALEX LOCKHEED
Transgender Romance
Meeting Jenna
Transgender Other
Being Sarah

BOOKS BY DIRK HESSIAN
Xtreme Historical Erotica
Ancient Times (Print only Bundle)*
The King's Men
Shores of Tripoli*
Prophecy of Noto
Pretender's Fate
General Historical Erotic Romance
Ridden West
Deliver a Virgin (Short)
Clouds and Rain (Short)
Confederate Gold
Puttin on the Ritz
To the Hessian Hills
Fire Down the Valley*
Constantinople*
The Beautiful Way*
Blue and Gray
Colonel's Treasure
Beginning of Time
Labyrinth

BOOKS BY HABU
Gay Erotica
Memoir Faction
Flying High, Diving Deep*
Xtreme Erotica
Fist of Gold

Liaisons
Chain Gang Banged (Short Story)
Tramp Steaming*
Escape to Girne
Silas' Choice*
Last Call
Choke Hold
Apyko: The Greek Pimp
Visits of the Schlange
Second Coming: Emile La Cour Unleashed*
Vortex: Sacrificed by Curiosity*
Dark Angel Sounding *(in e-book & included in Sounding:Ultimate
Control paperback)* *
Sounding: Ultimate Control (*Print Only*)*
Sounding Five *(in e-book & included in Sounding:Ultimate Control
paperback)* *

Romance
GayLords Inn*
Finding a New Sam
Bangkok Summer Seduction
The Photograph
Inevitable Case
Turn to Love
Rain Check
Built for Pleasure (Sci Fi)
Danny's Choice*
Pull of the Groove
Sugar n Spice Christmas
Friday Nights with Lenny (Christmas Romance)
Snowy, Snowy Nights (Christmas Romance)
Tank n Bull
Sail to the Sun
War Letters
Ravens Roost
Caribbean Cruise Top to Bottom
Arena Stage
Trading Partners (Valentine's Day)
Four Coins
Lower Than the Heart (Valentine's Day)
Brambleton
Gotta Keep Trying
Finding Amnad
Platres Conclave
Other Novels/Novellas
Another Frist Time

Syrian Ram
Temptation's Clutches*
Descent into Chaos
Escape to Girne
Journey Through Abilene
Harmony and Dissonance
Stallion Station
Racing With the Devil (espionage suspense)
Prepared in Cape Verdi
Gilded Cage
House on Park*
Anything for Ambition
Dance of the Ravishers
Hard Knocks U*
My Neighbor's Spa*
Man's Man: Tales of a High Priced Gay Hooker*
Trip Money
The Indian Doctor
Sailorboy
Home to Fire Island
Murder Mysteries
All Fools Day Foolery (Mike Kavanagh)
Inevitable Case (Mike Kavanagh)
Vanishing Laura
Death on a Ping Pong Table
Clint Folsom Mysteries Compendium Volume 1*
Death to Blonds - Stolen Judgment (Clint Folsom Mystery)*
Clint Folsom Mysteries Compendium Volume 2*
Gay Erotica Anthologies
Earth Cry*
Shunga
Habu's Christmas Balls
Eight in D*
DevilMENt
Silas' Choices*
Stallion Station (A Novella in Parts)
Eleven to the Dogs*
Fifty Seventy*
Spy Tails 001*
Spy Tails 002*
Doubled*
Doubled Again*
Tails in the Tropics*
Tails in the Med*
Tails in the West*

Rough Riders*
Grab Bag 1*
Grab Bag 2*
Grab Bag 3*
Grab Bag 4*
Grab Bag 5*
Grab Bag 6*
Grab Bag 7*
Grab Bag 8*
Grab Bag 9*
Grab Bag 10*
Beyond the Beaded Curtain*
Habu's Christmas Balls
The Sporting Life*
Fetish Galore!*
Literary Gay Erotica
Cairo Surrender*
The Handyman*
Homeward Bound
Journey to Mirage*
Bisexual/Menage/Multisexual Erotica
And Eat it Too
Two Men, One Woman*
Every Which Way
Summer of Denial
Death on a Ping Pong Table
Cruising Gigolo
13 Ways for Halloween
Luther*
The Indian Prince*
BOOKS BY SABB
Driver Reliever
Hiring in Hollywood
The Legend of Holleystone Grange
Surprise Encounters*
She is He
Wrong Man
Loyal to his King
Barbarian Tales - Book One - Traveler's Tales*
Barbarian Tales - Book Two - Journeys Begin*
Barbarian Tales - Book Three - The Inheritance*
Barbarian Tales - Book Four - Road to Persepolis*
BOOKS BY SHABBU
Velvet Interrogation
Finding Jason

Dirty Pool
Operation Black Jade
Cigars!*
Angel in the Barn
Gayly Complicated*
Despoiling David
The Tree of Idleness*
I Met a Man
Rough Road to Happiness
BOOKS BY STEPHEN KESSEL
Gay Romance
The Forever Man
Two Chances
BOOKS BY KIM BLACK
Lesbian Romance
Transfixed on Tammie (F/T lesbian)

www.ingramcontent.com/pod-product-compliance
Lightning Source LLC
Chambersburg PA
CBHW031344170626
46807CB00002B/823